Retold Classics

NOVELS

Frankenstein

Huckleberry Finn

The Red Badge
of Courage

The Scarlet Letter

A Tale of Two Cities

Treasure Island

ANTHOLOGIES

American Classics,
Volume 1

American Classics,
Volume 2

American Classics,
Volume 3

American Classics,
Nonfiction

American Hauntings

British Classics

Classic Chillers

Edgar Allan Poe

Jack London

Mark Twain

World Classics

The Retold Tales® Series features novels, short story
anthologies, and collections of myths and folktales.

Perfection Learning®

Alex Miller

Writer

Pat Perrin
Ph.D., Art Theory and Criticism
Educational Writer and Novelist

Consultants

Rhonda Fey
Educational Consultant
Des Moines, Iowa

Gretchen Kauffman
Educational Consultant
Des Moines, Iowa

Dr. Jona Mann
Educational Consultant
Madrid, Iowa

Lois Markham
Educational Writer
Beverly, Massachusetts

Retold Classics

Treasure Island

by Robert Louis Stevenson

Perfection Learning®

Senior Editor

Marsha James

Editors

Christine Rempe LePorte
Cecelia Munzenmaier

Cover Illustration

Mark Bischel

Inside Illustration

Frank McShane

Book Design

Dea Marks

For information contact
Perfection Learning® Corporation
1000 North Second Avenue, P.O. Box 500
Logan, Iowa 51546-0500
Phone: 1-800-831-4190 • Fax: 1-800-543-2745

Reinforced Library Binding ISBN-13: 978-0-7807-1704-6
Reinforced Library Binding ISBN-10: 0-7807-1704-X
Paperback ISBN-13: 978-1-5631-2264-4
Paperback ISBN-10: 1-5631-2264-2
13 14 15 16 17 PP 12 11 10 09 08
perfectionlearning.com
Printed in the U.S.A.

TABLE
OF CONTENTS

WELCOME TO THE RETOLD CLASSIC TREASURE ISLAND

Adventure, mischief, suspense, and unforgettable characters are but a few of the elements that help make Robert Louis Stevenson's *Treasure Island* a classic work.

We call something a classic when it is so well loved that it is saved and passed down to new generations. Classics have been around for a long time, but they're not dusty or out-of-date. That's because they are brought back to life by each new person who reads and enjoys them.

Treasure Island is a novel written years ago that continues to entertain and influence readers today. The story offers exciting plots, important themes, fascinating characters, and powerful language. This is a story that many people have loved to read and share with one another.

RETOLD UPDATE

The *Retold Classic Treasure Island* is different from Stevenson's original story in two ways.

- Some chapters have been omitted. Brief summaries are provided for these parts so you can follow the complete story.

- The language has been updated. All the colorful, gripping, or comic details of the original story are here. But longer sentences and paragraphs have been shortened or split up. And some old words have been replaced with modern language.

You will also find these special features. A word list has been added at the beginning of each chapter. The list should make reading easier. Each word defined on the list is printed in dark type within that chapter of the novel. If you forget the meaning of a word while you're reading, just check the list to review the definition.

In addition, you'll find a glossary and a ship diagram at the end of the book. The glossary defines most nautical terms that are used throughout the novel. And the different areas of a ship are labeled on the diagram to clarify some of these terms. Knowing these terms will make the novel even more meaningful for you.

You'll also see footnotes at the bottom of some pages. These notes identify people and places or explain words and ideas.

At the beginning of the book, you'll find a little information about Robert Louis Stevenson. These revealing facts will give you insight into his life and work.

One last word. If you feel compelled to read the entire story, we encourage you to locate an original version to get more of Stevenson's rich characterization and exciting plots.

Now on to the novel. Remember, when you read this book, you bring the story back to life in today's world. We hope you'll discover why this novel has earned the right to be called a literary classic.

Robert Louis Stevenson

INSIGHTS INTO
ROBERT LOUIS STEVENSON
(1850-1894)

From his childhood on, Robert Louis Balfour Stevenson loved adventure and travel. So it's not surprising that he wrote a book like *Treasure Island*. What is amazing is the fact that this story—along with many others—was written when he was very ill.

Stevenson suffered from a lung illness that began when he was a child. He spent much of his time in bed, but he wasn't bored. Instead, he passed his days making up exciting stories. And he read every book he could get his hands on.

Stevenson was born in Edinburgh, Scotland, to upper-middle-class parents. His father was a lighthouse engineer who pressured his son to follow the same path. For his father's sake, Stevenson attended the University of Edinburgh to study engineering. However, he had no interest in science, and his grades showed it. Besides, all he wanted to do was write.

Stevenson's father became angry at his son's apparent lack of ambition. The elder Stevenson felt that writing was a pastime, not a profession. After much arguing, father and son reached a compromise. Stevenson agreed to study law. And he would write only in his spare time.

In 1875, Stevenson passed his final bar exam and became a lawyer. But he was a lawyer in name only. He tried four minor cases. Then he decided to devote all his time to his first and only love—writing.

continued

His formal studies over, Stevenson traveled to the European mainland. He had two goals. The first was to get his writing career off the ground. The second was to find a climate suitable for his ill health.

For a long time it seemed neither goal would ever be realized. Though he wrote many articles, he sold few. His only income was a small allowance from his father. And his health didn't improve at all.

Something good did happen while Stevenson was in France. He met the woman of his dreams. She was an American woman named Fanny Osbourne. Osbourne was married, with two children. She had fled to Europe to escape a cruel husband. She supported herself and children with a small allowance her husband sent her. And she studied art, hoping for a career.

Though Osbourne was ten years older than Stevenson, they fell in love. The two spent much time together. Then Osbourne's husband threatened to cut off her money unless she returned to the United States.

Osbourne had no choice since she was making no money on her art work. And getting a divorce was not considered acceptable in the nineteenth century. So with her children, she returned to California.

Stevenson—who had never been healthy anyway— became even more ill with grief. At last he decided to follow his love to America. The trip was exhausting. He arrived at Osbourne's doorstep on the edge of death.

Seeing Stevenson again made Osbourne realize her true feelings. She nursed Stevenson back to health. And she decided to divorce her unfaithful husband, no matter what others thought of her. This accomplished, Stevenson and Osbourne were married at last.

The newlyweds remained in the United States until Stevenson was well enough to travel. Then they returned to Scotland, where the new Mrs. Stevenson met her in-laws for the first time. It proved a surprise to everyone when Fanny got along well with Stevenson's family. Stevenson's parents had been firmly against their son marrying an older, divorced woman.

However, Stevenson's friends resented his new wife. After all, she *was* a foreigner. And—according to them—she was entirely too protective of her husband. When they visited, she dared ask them to leave when Stevenson became tired. And sometimes she wouldn't even let her husband's friends see him at all.

However, Stevenson seemed to thrive under his wife's motherly care. He was never completely healthy. But he was well enough to produce some successful pieces of writing, the first of which was *Treasure Island*.

Stevenson got the idea for *Treasure Island* when he saw his stepson Lloyd drawing a picture of an island. Immediately Stevenson created a draft of the story inside his head. The tale of adventure excited him so much that he wrote a chapter a day.

Stevenson's father even became interested in the adventure tale. In fact, it was the elder Stevenson who decided on the contents of Billy Bones' chest. Apparently he had decided that if he couldn't fight his son's writing, he might as well join it.

At first it didn't seem the work would ever become a best-seller, much less a classic. Stevenson couldn't find a publisher willing to take it. He finally had to settle for having the story printed in serial form in a children's magazine called *Young Folks*. The original title for the work was *The Sea Cook*, and Stevenson didn't even use

continued

his own name. Instead, he used the pen name Captain George North.

Finally, the story was printed as a book under the name *Treasure Island*. It was published with Stevenson's own name on it. The book became a best-seller, and Stevenson was famous at last.

Riding on his success, Stevenson wrote another classic novel, *The Strange Case of Dr. Jekyll and Mr. Hyde.* This book—according to the author—was the result of a nightmare. One night Stevenson dreamed all the major scenes of the book. When he woke up, he immediately wrote down the main plot so he wouldn't forget it.

It is said that Stevenson wrote the entire book at a feverish pace, ignoring his ill health. Legend has it that at one point he wrote 25,000 words in three days. This is an almost impossible task even for someone in excellent health. Then—because his wife didn't like the book—he burned the entire work and wrote a second version just as quickly.

Eventually Stevenson's doctors sent him back to the United States. They hoped his health would improve there. Upon the Stevensons' arrival, a huge crowd awaited them. Stevenson soon realized that his fame in America was even greater than it was in Europe.

Unfortunately, he also found that many of his works had been stolen by U.S. publishers. These publishers printed Stevenson's books without paying him anything. Stevenson should have been one of the richest writers in the world. Instead, he was forced to write magazine articles to support his family.

In an attempt to aid Stevenson's health, his wife rented a yacht called the *Casco*. It was her intention that they should sail around the world. Maybe somewhere they would find the ideal climate for Stevenson's weak lungs.

It is said that when the boat's captain first saw the frail Stevenson, he prepared for a burial at sea.

When the ship was ready to sail, Stevenson, Fanny, her children, and Stevenson's mother set off for the South Seas. Stevenson loved sailing, and his health improved somewhat. The *Casco* toured the South Seas at a leisurely pace, stopping in Tahiti, Hawaii, and finally Samoa.

Stevenson didn't think much of the Samoan Islands at first. But soon he fell in love with the place and bought an estate on the island of Upolu. As he remarked to a friend, "I like this place better than any I have seen in the Pacific....Honolulu's good—very good, but this seems more savage."

It was in the South Seas that Stevenson's health was at its best. He also loved the Samoan people themselves. And the Samoans greatly respected the writer and admired his gentleness and wisdom. They treated him almost like a chief. The islanders called Stevenson *Tusitala,* which means "the teller of stories."

At first, Stevenson tried not to take sides in the conflicts between Samoa and the countries that controlled it—Germany, Britain, and the United States. But then the unfairness of colonial rule became evident to Stevenson. He began to speak out harshly against it. In time Stevenson identified himself more as a native Samoan than as a so-called white man.

Even in Samoa, Stevenson worked hard on his writing. Money was still tight, and his estate proved too expensive. Also, Stevenson supported more than his family. He was a generous man by nature. And he constantly sent money to his friends back home. He even gave away his money to some of the islanders.

continued

Stevenson wasn't fated to enjoy his new home for long. He was only forty-four when he died of a stroke in Samoa. But because of his writings—which include not only novels but poetry, travel books, short stories, and essays—Robert Louis Stevenson lives on today.

Other works by Stevenson
  Across the Plains, novel
  A Child's Garden of Verses, poetry collection
  Kidnapped, novel
  Memories and Portraits, essay collection
  New Arabian Nights, short story anthology
  The Strange Case of Dr. Jekyll and Mr. Hyde, novel

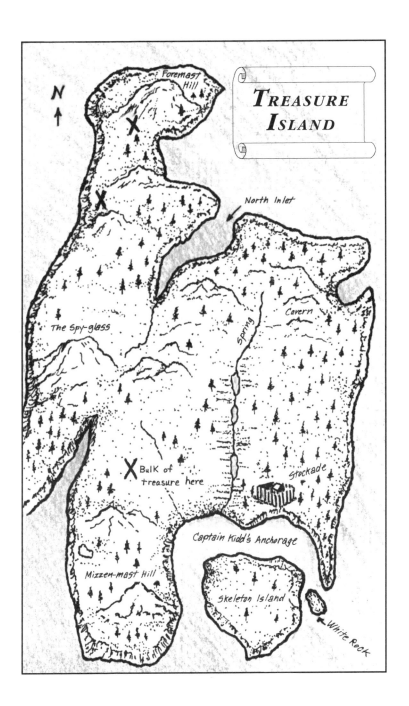

TREASURE ISLAND

by
Robert Louis Stevenson

PART I: THE OLD BUCCANEER[1]

Chapter 1

The Old Sea-Dog at the "Admiral Benbow"

Vocabulary Preview

The following words appear in this chapter. Review the list and get to know the words before you read the chapter.

annoyance—bother; nuisance
connoisseur—critic; specialist
contrast—difference
domineering—forceful; commanding

Squire Trelawney,[2] Dr. Livesey, and the rest of these gentlemen asked me to write down all the details about Treasure Island. They said to tell the story from beginning to end, keeping nothing back but the bearings of the island. And that was only because there is still treasure not yet dug up.

I take up my pen in the year of grace 17—.[3] I go back to the time when my father kept the "Admiral Benbow" inn. It was when the brown old seaman with the sabre cut[4]

---

[1] A buccaneer is a pirate.
[2] A squire is the owner of a large country estate. He is usually the major landowner in a village or district.
[3] Many early writers followed an old letter-writing custom of not writing a full date. This was done for privacy. Sometimes writers also used initials followed by dashes instead of full names.
[4] A sabre is a sword.

first took up his lodging under our roof.

I remember him as if it were yesterday. He came plodding to the inn door, his sea chest following along behind him in a wheelbarrow.

He was a tall, strong, heavy, nut-brown man. His black pigtail fell over the shoulders of his stained blue coat. His hands were ragged and scarred, with black, broken nails. The sabre cut across one cheek was a dirty, bluish white.

I remember him looking around the cove[5] and whistling to himself as he did so. Then he broke out in that old sea song that he sang so often afterwards:

"Fifteen men on the dead man's chest—
Yo-ho-ho, and a bottle of rum!"

His voice was high, old, and trembling. It seemed to have been tuned and broken at the capstan bars.[6]

Then he rapped on the door with a bit of a stick, that looked like a spike, which he carried. When my father appeared, the old sailor called roughly for a glass of rum. When it was brought to him, he drank it like a **connoisseur,** tasting it slowly. As he drank, he looked about him at the cliffs and up at our signboard.

"This is a handy cove," he said finally. "It's a pleasantly located grog-shop.[7] Much company, mate?"

My father told him no, very little company, the more was the pity.

"Well, then," said he, "this is the place for me. Here, you, matey," he cried to the man who pushed the wheelbarrow. "Bring that alongside and help me with my chest. I'll stay here a bit."

He continued talking to my father. "I'm a plain man. Rum and bacon and eggs is what I want, and that cliff up

---

[5] A cove is a small bay where the coastline curves inward and there is land on three sides.
[6] Most nautical terms used in the novel are defined in the glossary, which begins on page 191.
[7] Grog is rum and water or some other alcoholic drink and water. A grog shop is similar to a hotel or inn.

there to watch ships from. What might you call me? You might call me captain. Oh, I see what you're getting at— there." And he threw down three or four gold pieces in the doorway. "You can tell me when I've gone through that," he said, looking as fierce as a commander.

The old sailor's clothes were ragged and he spoke roughly. But, indeed, he did not look like an ordinary sailor. He seemed like a mate or skipper, used to being obeyed or striking out.

The man with the wheelbarrow told us the mail boat had set the captain down the morning before at the "Royal George." The captain had inquired what inns there were along the coast. I suppose he heard ours well spoken of and described as lonely. So he had chosen it over the others for his place of residence. And that was all we could learn about our guest.

He was a very silent man by habit. All day he hung round the cove or upon the cliffs with a brass telescope. All evening he sat in a corner of the parlor[8] next to the fire. There he drank rum and water very strong.

Mostly he would not speak when spoken to. He would just look up—suddenly and fiercely—and blow through his nose like a fog-horn. We and the people who came around our house soon learned to let him be.

Every day, when the captain came back from his walk, he would ask if any seafaring men[9] had gone by along the road. At first, we thought he asked this question because he wanted company of his own kind. But finally, we began to see he wanted to avoid them. When a seaman put up at the "Admiral Benbow"—some of them did, now and then, on their way to Bristol—the captain would look in at him through the curtained door before he entered the parlor. And he was always sure to be as silent as a mouse when any such man was present.

For me, at least, there was no secret about the matter.

[8] A parlor is a sitting room. In a hotel or inn, it is a room where guests can meet for conversation.
[9] A seafaring man is a sailor.

Alex Miller

In a way, I shared his alarms. He had taken me aside one day. He promised me a silver fourpenny[10] on the first of every month if I would only keep my eye open for a seafaring man with one leg. I was to let him know the moment such a man appeared.

When the first of each month came round, I asked the old captain for my wage. Often enough, he would only blow through his nose at me and stare me down. But before the week was out, he was sure to think better of it. He would bring me my fourpenny piece and repeat his orders to look out for the seafaring man with one leg.

How that person haunted my dreams, I hardly need tell you. I would dream of him especially on stormy nights. That was when the wind shook the four corners of the house, and the surf roared along the cove and up the cliffs. I would see the one-legged sailor in a thousand forms and with a thousand wicked expressions.

In my dreams, sometimes the leg would be cut off at the knee, another time at the hip. Next he was a monstrous kind of creature who had never had but the one leg—and that was in the middle of his body. To see him leap and run and chase me over hedges and ditches was the worst of nightmares. And, altogether, I paid pretty dearly for my monthly fourpenny piece in the form of these horrible fantasies.

I was terrified by the idea of the seafaring man with one leg. But I was far less afraid of the captain himself than anybody else who knew him. There were nights when he drank more rum and water than his head would carry. Then he would sometimes sit and sing his wicked, old, wild sea songs, paying attention to nobody.

But sometimes he would call for glasses of grog all around. Then he'd force all the trembling company to listen to his stories or to form the chorus to his singing. Often I've heard the house shaking with "Yo-ho-ho and a bottle of rum." All the neighbors joined in for dear life,

---

[10]A silver fourpenny was a British coin worth four pennies.

with the fear of death upon them. Each sang louder than the other, to avoid the captain's notice.

In these fits, the old sailor was the most **domineering** companion ever known. He would slap his hand on the table for silence all around. He'd fly up in a passion of anger at a question.

Sometimes he would even get mad when no question was asked. Then he figured that the company wasn't following his story. He wouldn't allow anyone to leave the inn till he had drunk himself sleepy and reeled off to bed.

The captain's stories were what frightened people worst of all. Dreadful stories they were—about hanging and walking the plank.[11] They were about storms at sea and the Dry Tortugas and wild deeds and places on the Spanish Main.[12] By his own account, the old sailor must have lived his life among some of the wickedest men that God ever allowed upon the sea.

The language in which he told these stories shocked our plain country people almost as much as the crimes that he described. My father was always saying the inn would be ruined. He thought people would soon stop coming there to be bullied and put down and sent shivering to their beds.

But I really believe the old sailor's presence did us good. People were frightened at the time, but on looking back I think they rather liked it. It was a fine excitement in a quiet country life.

There was even a group of the younger men who pretended to admire the captain. They called him a "true sea-dog" and a "real old salt"[13] and such names. They said there was the sort of man that made England fearful at sea.

[11]*Walking the plank* is being forced to walk, usually blindfolded, off a narrow board that hangs over the side of a ship and into the sea. Legends about pirates often feature captives being forced to walk the plank. However, there is no evidence that such a thing actually happened. It is certain that pirates did sometimes throw captives overboard to die.

[12]The Dry Tortugas are a small group of islands south of Florida. The Spanish Main is the northeast coast of South America and the nearby part of the Caribbean Sea.

[13]An old salt is an experienced sailor.

In one way, indeed, the captain almost ruined us. He kept on staying week after week and then month after month. All the money he paid us had been long used up. And still my father never got up the courage to insist on having more.

Whenever my father mentioned it, the captain blew through his nose so loudly that you might say he roared. He stared my poor father out of the room. I've seen my father wringing his hands after such an insult. I'm sure the **annoyance** and the terror he lived in must have greatly hurried his early and unhappy death.

All the time he lived with us, the captain made no change whatever in his dress. Except he did buy some stockings from a salesman. One of the cocks of his hat fell down.[14] He let it hang from that day on, though it was a great annoyance when the wind blew.

I remember the appearance of his coat. He patched it himself upstairs in his room. Before the end, it was nothing but patches.

He never wrote or received a letter. He never spoke with anyone but the neighbors. And for the most part, he only spoke with them when he was drunk on rum. The great sea chest none of us had ever seen open.

The captain was only once crossed, and that was towards the end. My poor father was far gone in an illness that took him off. Dr. Livesey came late one afternoon to see the patient. Then the doctor took a bit of dinner from my mother and went into the parlor to smoke a pipe. He was waiting for his horse to come down from the village, for we had no stables at the old "Benbow."

I followed the doctor into the parlor. I remember observing the **contrast** the neat, bright doctor made with the awkward country folk. The powder on the doctor's wig[15] was as white as snow. He had bright, black eyes and

---

[14]The edge of a cocked hat is pointed in three places. So the edge, or brim, is shaped like a triangle. One of the points on the captain's hat hung down and flopped in the wind.

[15]At the time the story takes place, professionals often wore powdered wigs in public.

pleasant manners. He contrasted, above all, with that filthy, heavy, watery-eyed scarecrow of a pirate of ours. The captain was sitting far gone in rum, with his arms on the table.

Suddenly he—the captain that is—began to pipe up his everlasting song:

"Fifteen men on the dead man's chest—
Yo-ho-ho, and a bottle of rum!
Drink and the devil had done for the rest—
Yo-ho-ho, and a bottle of rum!"

At first I had supposed "the dead man's chest" to be that same big box of his upstairs in the front room. The thought had been mixed in my nightmares with that of the one-legged seafaring man. But by this time, we had all long stopped paying any particular notice to the song. It was only new that night to Dr. Livesey.

I saw that the song did not produce an agreeable effect on the doctor. He looked up for a moment quite angrily. Then he went on with his talk to old Taylor, the gardener, on a new cure for the rheumatics.[16]

In the meantime, the captain gradually brightened up at his own music. At last he flapped his hand upon the table before him in a way we all knew to mean—silence.

The voices stopped at once, all but Dr. Livesey's. He went on as before, speaking clear and kind. He drew briskly at his pipe between every word or two.

The captain glared at him for a while, flapped his hand again, and glared still harder. At last he broke out with a wicked low oath, "Silence there, between decks!"

"Were you addressing me, sir?" said the doctor.

With another oath, the rascal told him that this was so.

"I have only one thing to say to you, sir," replied the doctor. "If you keep on drinking rum, the world will soon be rid of a very dirty scoundrel!"

---

[16]*Rheumatics* is now called "rheumatism." It can be any of a ꞏ ꞏber of conditions that cause pain in the joints or muscles.

The old captain's fury was awful. He sprang to his feet and drew out and opened a sailor's clasp-knife.[17] Balancing it open on the palm of his hand, he threatened to pin the doctor to the wall.

The doctor never so much as moved. He spoke to the captain, as before, over his shoulder and in the same tone of voice. He spoke rather loudly, so that all the room might hear. But his voice was perfectly calm and steady.

"Put that knife in your pocket this instant. If you don't, I promise, upon my honor, that you shall hang at the next court session."

Then followed a battle of looks between them. But the captain soon knuckled under. He put up his weapon and took his seat, grumbling like a beaten dog.

"And now, sir," continued the doctor to the captain. "Since I now know there's such a fellow in my district, I'll have an eye upon you day and night. You can count on it. I'm not only a doctor. I'm a magistrate.[18] If I hear a breath of complaint against you, I'll do what it takes to have you hunted down and routed out. Even if it's only for a piece of rudeness like tonight's. Let that be enough."

Soon after that, Dr. Livesey's horse came to the door, and the doctor rode away. But the captain held his peace that evening and for many evenings to come.

---

[17]A clasp-knife is a folding knife. It has a catch to hold the blade in the open position.
[18]A magistrate is similar to a judge. He or she has the power to carry out the law and to hold court.

Chapter 2

Black Dog Appears and Disappears

Vocabulary Preview

The following words appear in this chapter. Review the list and get to know the words before you read the chapter.

fawning—showing affection or flattery
fugitive—runaway; one who flees
indignation—anger; displeasure
prophetic—telling of a future event

It wasn't very long after this that the first of some mysterious events occurred. These were the events that would rid us at last of the captain. Though as you will see, they did not rid us of his affairs.

It was a bitter cold winter with long, hard frosts and heavy winds. It was plain from the first that my poor father was unlikely to see the spring. He got worse daily, and my mother and I had all the inn on our hands. We were kept busy enough without paying much attention to our unpleasant guest.

It was one January morning, very early—a pinching, frosty morning. The cove was all gray with frost. The ripples lapped softly on the stones. The sun was still low and only touching the hilltops and shining far out to sea.

The captain had risen earlier than usual and set out for the beach. His cutlass[1] was swinging under the broad skirts of the old blue coat. His brass telescope was under his arm, and his hat tilted back upon his head.

---

[1] A cutlass is a short sword with a curved blade.

I remember the captain's breath hanging like smoke behind him as he strode off. The last sound I heard of him, as he went around the big rock, was a snort of **indignation.** It was as though he still had his mind on Dr. Livesey.

Well, Mother was upstairs with Father, and I was laying the breakfast table for the captain's return. The parlor door opened and a man stepped in. I had never set my eyes on him before. He was a pale, waxy-faced creature, with two fingers missing on his left hand. Though he wore a cutlass, he didn't look much like a fighter.

I always had my eye open for seafaring men, with one leg or two. I remember this one puzzled me. He was not sailorlike. Yet he had the look of the sea about him too.

I asked what I might serve him, and he said he would take rum. But as I was going out of the room to fetch it, he sat down upon a table and motioned me to draw near. I paused where I was, with my napkin in my hand.

"Come here, sonny," said he. "Come nearer here."

I took a step nearer.

"Is this here table for my mate Bill?" he asked, with a kind of leer.

I told him I didn't know his mate Bill. I said this was for a person who stayed in our house, whom we called the captain.

"Well," said he, "my mate Bill would be called the captain, likely as not. He has a cut on one cheek. And he has a mighty pleasant way with him, especially when he's drinking. For argument's sake we'll put it that your captain has a cut on one cheek. And we'll put it—if you like—that that cheek's the right one. Ah, well! I told you. Now, is my mate Bill in this here house?"

I told him he was out walking.

"Which way, sonny? Which way has he gone?"

I pointed out the rock. I told him the way the captain was likely to return and how soon and answered a few other questions.

"Ah," said he, "this'll be as good as drink to my mate Bill."

The expression on his face as he said these words was not at all pleasant. And I had my own reasons for thinking that the stranger was mistaken about the captain's reaction. That was even supposing the stranger meant what he said. But it was no business of mine, I thought. Besides, it was difficult to know what to do.

The stranger kept hanging about just inside the inn door. He peered around the corner like a cat waiting for a mouse. Once I stepped out into the road myself, but he immediately called me back. When I didn't obey quick enough for his taste, a most horrible change came over his waxy face. He ordered me in with an oath[2] that made me jump.

As soon as I was back again, he returned to his former manner. Half **fawning,** half sneering, he patted me on the shoulder. He told me I was a good boy and he had taken quite a fancy to me.

"I have a son of my own," said he, "as like you as two blocks. He's all the pride of my heart. But the great thing for boys is discipline, sonny—discipline. Now, if you had sailed along with Bill, you wouldn't have stood there to be spoke to twice—not you. That was never Bill's way, nor the way of the men that sailed with him.

"And here, sure enough, is my mate Bill with a spy-glass under his arm. Bless his old heart, to be sure. You and me'll just go back into the parlor, sonny, and get behind the door. We'll give Bill a little surprise—bless his heart, I say again."

So saying, the stranger backed along with me into the parlor. He put me behind him in the corner so that we were both hidden by the open door. I was very uneasy and alarmed, as you might imagine.

It rather added to my fears to notice that the stranger was certainly frightened himself. He cleared the handle of

[2] *Oath* in this context means "swearing."

his cutlass and loosened the blade in the sheath.[3] All the time we were waiting there, he kept swallowing as if he felt what we used to call a lump in the throat.

At last, in strode the captain. He slammed the door behind him, without looking to the right or left. He marched straight across the room to where his breakfast awaited him.

"Bill," said the stranger in a voice that I thought he had tried to make bold and big.

The captain spun around on his heel and faced us. All the brown had gone out of his face. Even his nose was blue. He had the look of a man who sees a ghost or the evil one, or something worse, if anything can be. Upon my word, I felt sorry to see him turn so old and sick all at once.

"Come, Bill, you know me. You know an old shipmate, Bill, surely," said the stranger.

The captain made a sort of gasp.

"Black Dog!" said he.

"And who else?" replied the other, getting more at ease. "Black Dog as ever was, come to see his old shipmate Billy at the 'Admiral Benbow' inn. Ah, Bill, Bill, we've seen a sight of times, us two, since I lost them two claws." He held up his mangled hand.

"Now look here," said the captain. "You've run me down. Here I am. Well, then, speak up. What is it?"

"That's you, Bill," replied Black Dog. "You're in the right of it, Billy. I'll have a glass of rum from this dear child here that I've took such a liking to. If you please, we'll sit down and talk square, like old shipmates."

When I returned with the rum, they were already seated on either side of the captain's breakfast table. Black Dog was next to the door. He sat sideways, so as to have one eye on his old shipmate and one, I thought, on his escape.

Black Dog told me to go and to leave the door wide open. "None of your peeking through the keyholes for

---

[3] A sheath is a case for a knife or sword.

me, sonny," he said.

I left them together and went into the bar.

For a long time, I certainly did my best to listen. I could hear nothing but a low gabbling. But at last the voices began to grow louder. Then I could pick up a word or two—mostly oaths—from the captain.

"No, no, no, no, and an end of it!" the captain cried once. And again, "If it comes to swinging, swing all, say I."[4]

Then all of a sudden there was a great explosion of oaths and other noises. The chair and table went over in a lump. A clash of steel followed and then a cry of pain. The next instant I saw Black Dog in full flight and the captain hotly pursuing him. Both had drawn their cutlasses and Black Dog had blood streaming from the left shoulder.

Just at the door, the captain aimed one last tremendous cut at the **fugitive.** It would certainly have split him to the backbone if it hadn't been blocked by our big signboard of "Admiral Benbow." You can see the notch on the lower side of the frame to this day.

That blow was the last of the battle. Once out on the road, Black Dog showed a wonderfully clean pair of heels in spite of his wound. He disappeared over the edge of the hill in half a minute. For his part, the captain stood staring at the signboard like a dazed man. Then he passed his hand over his eyes several times. At last he turned back into the house.

"Jim," said he, "rum." As he spoke, he reeled a little and caught himself with one hand against the wall.

"Are you hurt?" I cried.

"Rum," he repeated. "I must get away from here. Rum! Rum!"

I ran to fetch it, but I was quite unsteady from all that had happened. I broke one glass and spilled the rum. While I was still getting in my own way, I heard a loud fall

---

[4] *Swinging* means "hanging." Many crimes, such as robbery and piracy, were punished by hanging.

in the parlor. Running in, I found the captain lying full length upon the floor.

At the same instant, my mother came running downstairs to help me. She had been alarmed by the cries and the fighting. Between us we raised the captain's head. He was breathing very loud and hard. But his eyes were closed and his face a was horrible color.

"Dear, deary me," cried my mother. "What a disgrace upon the house! And your poor father sick!"

In the meantime, we had no idea what to do to help the captain. We thought he had got his death-hurt in the scuffle with the stranger. I got the rum, to be sure, and tried to put it down his throat. But his teeth were tightly shut and his jaws as strong as iron.

It was a happy relief for us when the door opened and Doctor Livesey came in. He was on his way to visit my father.

"Oh, doctor," we cried, "what shall we do? Where is he wounded?"

"Wounded? Fiddlesticks,"[5] said the doctor. "He is no more wounded than you or I. The man has had a stroke,[6] as I warned him. Now, Mrs. Hawkins, you just run upstairs to your husband. If possible, tell him nothing about it. For my part, I must do my best to save this fellow's worthless life. Jim here will get me a bowl."

When I got back with the bowl, the doctor had already ripped up the captain's sleeve. He exposed the captain's great strong arm. It was tattooed in several places—"Here's luck," "A fair wind," and "Billy Bones his fancy." Those tattoos were neatly and clearly drawn on the forearm. Up near the shoulder there was a sketch of a gallows[7] and a man hanging from it. I thought that was done with great spirit.

"Prophetic," said the doctor, touching this picture with his finger. "And now, Master Billy Bones—if that be

---

[5] *Fiddlesticks* means "nonsense."
[6] A stroke is a sudden bursting of an artery in the brain.
[7] A gallows is a structure used for hanging criminals.

your name—we'll have a look at the color of your blood. Jim," he said, "are you afraid of blood?"

"No, sir," said I.

"Well, then," said he, "you hold the bowl." And with that, he took his lancet and opened a vein.[8]

A great deal of blood was taken before the captain opened his eyes and looked foggily about him. First he recognized the doctor with an unmistakable frown. Then his glance fell upon me, and he looked relieved. But suddenly his color changed.

The captain tried to raise himself, crying out, "Where's Black Dog?"

"There is no Black Dog here," said the doctor, "except what you have on your own back. You have been drinking rum. You have had a stroke, exactly as I told you. I have just—very much against my own will—dragged you headfirst out of the grave. Now, Mr. Bones—"

"That's not my name," the captain interrupted.

"Much I care," replied the doctor. "It's the name of a buccaneer that I know. I call you by it for the sake of shortness. What I have to say to you is this: one glass of rum won't kill you. But if you take one, you'll take another and another. I bet my wig that if you don't break off short, you'll die. Do you understand that? You'll die and go to your own place, like the man in the Bible.[9] Come, now, make an effort. I'll help you to your bed for once."

Between us—with much trouble—we managed to hoist the captain upstairs. We laid him on his bed. The captain's head fell back on the pillow, as if he were almost fainting.

"Now, mind you," said the doctor. "I clear my conscience—the name of rum for you is death."

And with that, he went off to see my father. He took me by the arm and brought me with him.

---

[8] A lancet is a knife used in surgery. Bleeding was an old medical treatment.
[9] "The man in the Bible" probably refers to Judas, one of Jesus' apostles. Judas betrayed Jesus and then hanged himself.

"This is nothing," the doctor said, as soon as he had closed the door. "I have drawn enough blood to keep him quiet for a while. He should lie for a week where he is—that's the best thing for him and you. But another stroke would finish him."

Chapter 3

The Black Spot

Vocabulary Preview

The following words appear in this chapter. Review the list and get to know the words before you read the chapter.

deformed—misshapen; twisted
mortal—great; extreme
reassured—given hope; supported
summons—signal; notice

About noon, I stopped at the captain's door with some cooling drinks and medicines. He was lying very much as we had left him, only a little livelier. He seemed both weak and excited.

"Jim," he said, "you're the only one here that's worth anything. And you know I've always been good to you. Every month I've given you a silver fourpenny for yourself. Now you see, mate, I'm feeling pretty low and deserted by all. Jim, you'll bring me one little mug of rum, now, won't you, mate?"

"The doctor—" I began.

But the captain broke in, cursing the doctor in a weak but hearty voice.

"Doctors is all swabs,"[1] he said. "And that doctor there, why what do he know about seafaring men? I been in places hot as pitch, with mates dropping around me with Yellow Jack.[2] And the blessed land heaving like the sea with earthquakes.

[1] A swab is a sailor. The word is also used to mean "worthless person."
[2] Yellow Jack is yellow fever, a tropical disease that is carried by mosquitoes.

"What do the doctor know of lands like that?" continued the captain. "I lived on rum, I tell you. Rum's been meat and drink and man and wife to me. If I'm not to have my rum now, I'm a poor old hulk on a lee shore. My blood'll be on you, Jim, and on that doctor swab."

He ran on again for a while with curses. "Look, Jim, how my fingers fidget," he continued in the pleading tone. "I can't keep 'em still, not I. I haven't had a drop this blessed day. That doctor's a fool, I tell you.

"If I don't have a drink o' rum, Jim," the old seaman went on, "I'll have the horrors. I seen some of 'em already. I seen old Flint there in the corner behind you. I seen him as plain as print. If I get the horrors, I'm a man that has lived rough and I'll raise Cain. Your doctor hisself said one glass wouldn't hurt me. I'll give you a golden guinea[3] for a little mug, Jim."

He was growing more and more excited. This made me feel alarmed for my father, who was very ill that day and needed quiet. I was **reassured** by the doctor's words, now quoted to me. But I was rather offended by the offer of a bribe.

"I want none of your money," said I, "except what you owe my father. I'll get you one glass and no more."

When I brought it to him, he seized it greedily and drank it up.

"Ay, ay," said he, "that's some better, sure enough. And now, matey, did that doctor say how long I was to lie here in this old bed?"

"A week at least," said I.

"Thunder!" he cried. "A week! I can't do that. They'd have the black spot on me by then. The lubbers[4] is trying to catch up with me this blessed moment. Those lubbers couldn't keep what they got and they want to nail what is another's. Is that seamanly behavior, now, I want to know?

"But I'm a saving soul," he went on. "I never wasted

---

[3] A guinea was a British gold coin.
[4] A lubber is a worthless person. *Lubber* is also slang for "sailor."

good money of mine, nor lost it neither. I'll trick 'em again. I'm not afraid of 'em. I'll shake out another reef,[5] matey, and leave 'em behind again."

As he was speaking, he had risen from bed with great difficulty. He held onto my shoulder with a grip that almost made me cry out. He moved his legs like so much dead weight. As lively as his words were in meaning, they contrasted sadly with the weak voice in which they were said. He paused when he got into a sitting position on the edge.

"That doctor's done me," he murmured. "My ears is singing. Lay me back."

Before I could do much to help him, he had fallen back again to his former place. He lay there for a while, silent.

"Jim," he said, at length, "you saw that seafaring man today?"

"Black Dog?" I asked.

"Ah! Black Dog," said he. *"He's* a bad one. But the men that sent him are worse. Now, mind you, if I can't get away any how and they give me the black spot, it's my old sea chest they're after. You get on a horse—you can, can't you? Well, then, you get on a horse and go to—well, yes, I will! Go to that eternal doctor swab and tell him to pipe all hands[6]—magistrates and such. He'll find 'em at the 'Admiral Benbow'—all old Flint's crew, man and boy, all of 'em that's left.

"I was first mate, I was," the captain said, "old Flint's first mate. And I'm the only one that knows the place. Flint gave it to me at Savannah,[7] when he lay a-dying— like as if I was to now, you see. But you won't go telling anyone this unless they get the black spot on me. Or unless you see that Black Dog again or a seafaring man with one leg, Jim—him above all."

"But what is the black spot, captain?" I asked.

---

[5] *Shake out another reef* means "get up more speed."

[6] A ship captain's orders could be announced by playing signals on a pipe. One such signal ordered all sailors to gather on the ship's deck.

[7] Savannah is a seaport on the Georgia coast.

"That's a **summons,** mate. I'll tell you if they get that to me. But you keep your eye open, Jim, and I'll share with you equals, upon my honor."

He spoke a little longer, his voice growing weaker. He took his medicine like a child, with the remark, "If ever a seaman wanted drugs, it's me."

Soon after I gave him the medicine, he fell at last into a heavy sleep. It was almost as though he had passed out. I left him like that. What I would have done if all had gone well, I do not know. Probably I would have told the whole story to the doctor. I was in **mortal** fear that the captain might regret his confessions and make an end of me.

But as things happened, my poor father died quite suddenly that evening. That put all other matters aside. Our natural distress, the visits of the neighbors, and the arranging of the funeral kept me busy. And all the work of the inn had to be carried on meanwhile. I hardly had time to think of the captain, far less to be afraid of him.

The captain got downstairs the next morning, to be sure. He had his meals as usual, though he ate little. I'm afraid he had more than his usual supply of rum. He helped himself out of the bar, scowling and blowing through his nose. No one dared to cross him.

On the night before the funeral, the captain was as drunk as ever. In that house of mourning, it was shocking to hear him singing away at his ugly old sea song. But weak as he was, we all feared death for him. And the doctor was suddenly taken up with a case many miles away. He was never near the house after my father's death.

I have said the captain was weak. And indeed he seemed to grow weaker rather than regain his strength. He climbed up and down stairs and went from the parlor to the bar and back again. Sometimes he put his nose out of doors to smell the sea. As he went he held on to the walls for support. He breathed hard and fast like a man on a steep mountain.

The captain never spoke directly to me. It is my belief he had as good as forgotten his confessions to me. But his temper was more changeable and—allowing for his bodily weakness—more violent than ever. He had an alarming habit now when he was drunk. He would draw his cutlass and lay it bare before him on the table.

But, with all that, he paid less attention to people. He seemed shut up in his own wandering thoughts. Once, for instance, he sang a different tune, to our extreme wonder. It was a kind of country love song. The captain must have learned it in his youth before he had begun to follow the sea.

So things passed until the day after the funeral. It was about three o'clock on a bitter, foggy, frosty afternoon. I was standing at the door for a moment, full of sad thoughts about my father. I saw someone drawing slowly near along the road. He was plainly blind, for he tapped before him with a stick and wore a great green shade over his eyes and nose.

The blind man was bent over, as if with age or weakness. He wore a huge old tattered sea cloak with a hood, which made him appear positively **deformed.** I never in my life saw a more dreadful-looking figure. He stopped a little way from the inn. Raising his voice in an odd sing-song, he spoke to the air in front of him.

"Will any kind friend inform a poor blind man where or in what part of this country he may now be? He has lost the precious sight of his eyes in the gracious defense of his native country, England. And God bless King George!"

"You are at the 'Admiral Benbow' in Black Hill Cove, my good man," said I.

"I hear a voice," said he, "a young voice. Will you give me your hand, my kind young friend, and lead me in?"

I held out my hand, and the horrible, soft-spoken, eyeless creature gripped it in a moment like a vise. I was so much startled that I struggled to withdraw. But the blind man pulled me up close to him with a single action of his arm.

"Now, boy," he said, "take me in to the captain."

"Sir," said I, "upon my word I dare not."

"Oh," he sneered, "that's it! Take me in straight or I'll break your arm."

And as he spoke he gave my arm a twist that made me cry out.

"Sir," I said, "it is for yourself I mean. The captain isn't what he used to be. He sits with a drawn cutlass. Another gentleman—"

"Come now, march," interrupted he. I never heard a voice so cruel and cold and ugly as that blind man's. It frightened me more than the pain, and I began to obey him at once. I walked straight in at the door and towards the parlor. Our sick old buccaneer was sitting there, dazed with rum.

The blind man clung close to me, holding me in one iron fist. He leaned almost more of his weight on me than I could carry.

"Lead me straight up to him," the blind man said. "When I'm in view, cry out 'Here's a friend for you, Bill.' If you don't, I'll do this."

With that, he gave me a twitch that I thought would have made me faint. Between this and that, I was so completely terrified of the blind beggar that I forgot my terror of the captain. As I opened the parlor door, I cried out in a trembling voice the words the blind man had ordered.

The poor captain raised his eyes. At one look, the rum went out of him and left him staring sober. The expression on his face was not so much of terror as of mortal sickness. He made a movement to rise. But I don't believe he had enough force left in his body.

"Now, Bill, sit where you are," said the beggar. "Even if I can't see, I can hear a finger stirring. Business is business. Hold out your right hand. Boy, take his right hand by the wrist and bring it near to my right."

We both obeyed him to the letter. I saw the blind man pass something from the hollow of the hand that held his stick into the palm of the captain's. The captain's hand closed upon it instantly.

"And now that's done," said the blind man. At the words he suddenly let go of me. With incredible accuracy and nimbleness, he skipped out of the parlor and into the road. As I still stood motionless, I could hear his stick go tap-tap-tapping into the distance.

It was some time before either I or the captain seemed to gather our senses. At last, I released his wrist, which I was still holding. At the same moment, he drew in his hand and looked sharply into the palm.

"Ten o'clock!" he cried. "Six hours. We'll do them yet."

The captain sprang to his feet. Even as he did so, he reeled and put his hand to his throat. He stood swaying for a moment. Then, with a strange sound, he fell from his whole height face-first to the floor.

I ran to him at once, calling to my mother. But haste was all in vain. The captain had been struck dead by thundering apoplexy.[8]

As soon as I saw that he was dead, I burst into a flood of tears. It is a curious thing to understand. I had certainly never liked the man, though lately I had begun to pity him. But it was the second death I had known, and the sorrow of the first was still fresh in my heart.

---

[8] Apoplexy is a stroke. The rupture of an artery in the brain causes a sudden loss of feeling or movement. It can also cause death.

Chapter 4 (Summary)

The Sea Chest

When Jim told his mother the whole story, they both knew they were in a dangerous position. Some of the captain's money—if he had any—was owed to the innkeepers for his unpaid bill. But Jim and his mother were afraid that Black Dog or the blind beggar would soon return. Jim didn't think that the captain's old shipmates would give up their booty[1] to pay the debt.

If Jim rode to see Dr. Livesey, his mother would be left alone. So mother and son went to the nearby village, but no one there would help them. The name of Captain Flint—the man the dead captain had sailed under—was well known and greatly feared in the village.

Jim and his mother went back to the inn. They were determined to open the captain's chest and claim their money. Jim locked the door and closed the blinds. The dead captain still lay there on the parlor floor. In his hand was a round piece of paper, colored black—the black spot. On the other side of the paper was written, "You have till ten tonight."

To their relief, it was only six o'clock. Jim found a key hanging on a chain around the dead man's neck. He and his mother hurried upstairs and unlocked the sea chest. Beneath many other items, they found a bundle of papers tied up in oilcloth.[2] They also found a canvas bag full of coins from many countries.

Jim's mother began to count out the money that was owed to them. Then Jim heard a terrifying sound—the tap-tapping noise of the blind man's stick on the frozen road. Jim and his mother heard the man try the inn door, which was bolted. After a frightening period of silence,

[1] Booty is stolen goods or loot.
[2] Oilcloth is a fabric, such as canvas, that has been treated with oil to make it waterproof.

they at last heard the cane tap-tapping away again.

Jim urged his mother to take all the money and leave. But she wanted exactly what was owed to her, no more or less. In the middle of their arguing they heard a low whistle off in the hills. The seamen were coming to the inn!

Jim and his mother took the coins already counted. Jim grabbed the oilskin packet—"to square the count"— and they fled. They were less than halfway to the village when they heard footsteps and saw a bouncing light. Men were moving toward them with a lantern.

Jim and his mother had reached a small bridge. Although his mother fainted, Jim managed to drag her down the bank and partly under the bridge. He crawled under the low space. He knew that his mother could be seen if anybody looked closely. And they were still within earshot of the inn.

Chapter 5

The Last of the Blind Man

Vocabulary Preview

The following words appear in this chapter. Review the list and get to know the words before you read the chapter.

appeal—emotional request; plea
assault—attack
astonishment—surprise
formidable—fearful; forceful
hailed—called out to; signaled

In a sense, my curiosity was stronger than my fear. I could not remain where I was, but crept back to the bank again. There, hiding my head behind a bush, I could see the road in front of our door. I was barely in position before my enemies began to arrive.

All seven or eight of them came running hard, their feet beating out of time along the road. The man with the lantern was some paces in front. Three men ran together hand in hand. Even through the mist I made out that the middle man of this threesome was the blind beggar. The next moment his voice showed me that I was right.

"Down with the door," he cried.

"Aye, aye, sir!" answered two or three.

A rush was made upon the "Admiral Benbow." The lantern-bearer followed. Then I could see them pause. I heard speech in low voices, as if they were surprised to find the door open. But the pause was brief, for the blind man again gave his commands. His voice sounded louder and higher, as if he were fired up with eagerness and rage.

"In, in, in!" he shouted, and cursed them for their delay.

Four or five of them obeyed at once. Two of them remained in the road with the **formidable** beggar. There was a pause, then a cry of surprise, and then a voice shouting from the house.

"Bill's dead!"

But the blind man swore at them again for their delay.

"Search him, some of you lazy lubbers. The rest of you go up and get the chest," he cried.

I could hear their feet rattling up our old stairs. The house must have shook with it. Promptly afterwards, new sounds of **astonishment** arose. The window of the captain's room was thrown open with a slam and a jingle of broken glass. A man leaned out into the moonlight, head and shoulders. He addressed the blind beggar on the road below him.

"Pew," he cried, "they've been before us. Someone's turned the chest out low and high."

"Is it there?" roared Pew.

"The money's there."

The blind man cursed the money.

"Flint's fist, I mean," he cried.

"We don't see it here, nohow," replied the man.

"Here, you below there. Is it on Bill?" cried the blind man again.

At that, another fellow came to the door of the inn. He was probably the one who had remained below to search the captain's body.

"Bill's been gone over already," said he. "Nothin' left."

"It's these people of the inn—it's that boy. I wish I had put his eyes out!" cried the blind man, Pew. "They were here no time ago. They had the door bolted when I tried it. Scatter, lads, and find 'em."

"Sure enough, they left their candle burning here," said the fellow from the window.

"Scatter and find 'em! Rout the house out!" repeated

Pew, striking with his stick upon the road.

Then there followed a great to-do all through our old inn. Heavy feet pounded to and fro. Furniture was thrown over and doors kicked in until the very rocks echoed. The men came out again, one after another, on the road. They declared that we were nowhere to be found.

Just then, a whistle was clearly heard in the night. It was the same whistle that had alarmed my mother and me over the dead captain's money. But this time it was repeated twice.

Before, I had thought it to be the blind man's trumpet, so to speak. I had thought he was calling his crew to the **assault**. Now I found that it was a signal from the hillside near the village. From the effect on the buccaneers, it was a signal to warn them of coming danger.

"There's Dirk again," said one. "Twice! We'll have to move, mates."

"Move, you sneak!" cried Pew. "Dirk was a fool and a coward from the first. Don't mind him. Those inn people must be close by. They can't be far. You have your hands on it. Scatter and look for them, dogs! Oh, shiver my soul,"[1] he cried, "if I had eyes!"

This **appeal** seemed to produce some effect. Two of the fellows began to look here and there among the lumber. But they did so halfheartedly, I thought. They had half an eye to their own danger all the time. The others stood undecided on the road.

"You have your hands on thousands, you fools, and you hang back! You'd be as rich as kings if you could find it. You know it's here and you stand there loafing about. There wasn't one of you dared face Bill. And I did it—a blind man!

"And I'm to lose my chance because of you!" he went on. "I'm to be a poor, crawling beggar, sponging for

---

[1] In this phrase, *shiver* means "to shatter or splinter." "Shiver my soul," "shiver my sides," and "shiver my timbers" were phrases used by sailors in many stories and plays. They may or may not have an actual nautical origin.

rum—when I might be rolling in a coach! If you had the pluck of a weevil in a biscuit[2] you'd catch them still."

"Hang it, Pew, we've got the doubloons!"[3] grumbled one.

"They might have hid the blessed thing," said another. "Take the coins, Pew, and don't stand here squalling."

Pew's anger rose so high at these objections that squalling was the word for it. At last his passion completely took the upper hand. He struck at them right and left in his blindness. His stick sounded heavily on more than one.

These, in their turn, cursed back at the blind villain. They threatened him in horrid terms. They tried in vain to catch the stick and yank it from his grasp.

This quarrel saved us. While it was raging, another sound came from the top of the hill on the side of the village—the tramp of horses galloping. Almost at the same time, the flash and report of a pistol shot came from the hedge side. And that was plainly the last signal of danger.

The buccaneers turned at once and ran, separating in every direction. One went seaward along the cove, one slanted across the hill, and so on.

In half a minute, not a sign of them remained but Pew. Him they deserted. Whether it was in sheer panic or out of revenge for his harsh words and blows, I know not. But there he remained behind. He tapped up and down the road in a frenzy, reaching out and calling for his comrades. Finally, he took the wrong turn and ran a few steps past me towards the village.

He cried, "Johnny, Black Dog, Dirk," and other names. "You won't leave old Pew, mates—not old Pew!"

Just then the noise of horses topped the hill. Four or five riders came in sight in the moonlight. They swept at full gallop down the slope.

---

[2] A weevil is a small beetle that eats flour and grains and other stored foods.
[3] Doubloons were Spanish gold coins.

At this, Pew saw his error. He turned with a scream and ran straight for the ditch, into which he rolled. But he was on his feet again in a second. Completely confused now, he made another dash—right under the nearest of the coming horses.

The rider tried to save him, but in vain. Down went Pew with a cry that rang high into the night. The four hoofs trampled and left him and passed by.

Pew fell on his side. Then he gently collapsed upon his face and moved no more.

I leaped to my feet and **hailed** the riders. At any rate they were pulling up, horrified at the accident.

I soon saw what they were. One, tailing out behind the rest, was a lad that had gone from the village to Dr. Livesey's. The rest were revenue officers.[4] The lad had met them along the way and had the intelligence to return with them at once.

Some news of the lugger in Kitt's Hole[5] had found its way to Supervisor Dance.[6] He had set out that night in our direction. To that, my mother and I owed our escape from death.

Pew was dead, stone dead. As for my mother, we carried her up to the village. And a little cold water and salts[7] soon brought her back again. She was none the worse for her terror, although she was still upset over the rest of the money.

In the meantime, the supervisor rode on as fast as he could to Kitt's Hole. But his men had to dismount and grope down the valley, sometimes leading and sometimes supporting their horses. They were in constant fear of being attacked. So it was no big surprise that when they got down to the Hole the lugger was already under way. But it was still close by.

The supervisor hailed her. A voice replied, telling him

[4] Revenue officers were tax collectors.
[5] Kitt's Hole was a local port where ships docked.
[6] A supervisor is an officer in charge of a government unit or operation.
[7] Sharp-smelling salts, often called smelling salts, are sniffed to revive a person who has fainted.

to keep out of the moonlight or he would get some lead in him. At the same time, a bullet whistled close by his arm. Soon after, the lugger rounded the point and disappeared. Mr. Dance stood there "like a fish out of water," as he said. All he could do was to send a man to B—— to warn the cutter.

"And that," said the supervisor, "is just about as good as nothing. They've got off clean, and there's an end. Only," he added—for by this time he had heard my story—"I'm glad I trod on Master Pew's corns."

I went back with him to the "Admiral Benbow." You cannot imagine a house in such a smashed-up state. The very clock had been thrown down by these fellows in their furious hunt after my mother and myself. Nothing had actually been taken away except the captain's money bag and a little silver from the drawer. However, I could see at once that we were ruined.

Mr. Dance could make nothing of the scene. "They got the money, you say? Well then, Hawkins, what in fortune were they after? More money, I suppose?"

"No, sir. Not money, I think," replied I. "In fact, sir, I believe I have the thing in my breast pocket. To tell you the truth, I should like to get it put in safety."

"To be sure, boy. Quite right," said he. "I'll take it, if you like."

"I thought perhaps Dr. Livesey—" I began.

"Perfectly right," he interrupted, very cheerily. "Perfectly right—a gentleman and a magistrate. And now I come to think of it, I might as well ride round there myself and report to him or the squire.

"Master Pew's dead, when all's done" continued Mr. Dance. "Not that I regret it, but he's dead, you see. People will hold it against an officer of his Majesty's revenue, if they can. Now, I tell you Hawkins, if you like I'll take you along."

I thanked him heartily for the offer and we walked back to the village where the horses were. By the time I had told Mother of my plans, they were all in the saddle.

"Dogger," said Mr. Dance, "you have a good horse. Take this lad up behind you."

As soon as I was mounted and holding on to Dogger's belt, the supervisor gave the word. The party struck out at a bouncing trot on the road to Dr. Livesey's house.

Chapter 6

The Captain's Papers

Vocabulary Preview

The following words appear in this chapter. Review the list and get to know the words before you read the chapter.

ambiguity—uncertainty; confusion
cache—hiding place
condescending—snobbish; self-important
plundered—robbed; stole
unintelligible—meaningless; not able to be understood

We rode hard all the way, till we drew up before Dr. Livesey's door. The house was all dark at the front.

Mr. Dance told me to jump down and knock. Dogger gave me a stirrup to descend by. The door was opened almost at once by the maid.

"Is Dr. Livesey in?" I asked.

No, she said. He had come home in the afternoon but had gone up to the Hall to dine and pass the evening with the squire.

"So there we go, boys," said Mr. Dance.

This time I didn't mount since the distance was short. I ran next to Dogger's stirrup-leather to the lodge gates and up the long, leafless moonlit avenue. The white line of the Hall buildings looked out on great old gardens on either side. Here Mr. Dance dismounted. Taking me along with him, he was admitted at a word into the house.

The servant led us down a passage that had mats on the floor. He showed us at the end into a great library, all lined with bookcases with busts[1] on top of them. The squire and Dr. Livesey sat there, pipe in hand, on either side of a bright fire.

I had never seen the squire so near at hand. He was a tall man—over six feet high—and broad in size. He had a hearty rough-and-ready face, all roughened and reddened and lined from his long travels. His eyebrows were very black and moved quickly. This gave him a look of some temper—not bad, you would say, but quick and high.

"Come in, Mr. Dance," said the squire, very dignified and **condescending.**

"Good evening, Dance," said the doctor with a nod. "And good evening to you, friend Jim. What good wind brings you here?"

The supervisor stood up straight and stiff and told his story like a lesson. You should have seen how the two gentlemen leaned forward and looked at each other. They forgot to smoke in their surprise and interest.

When they heard how my mother went back to the inn, Dr. Livesey fairly slapped his thigh. The squire cried "Bravo!" and broke his long pipe against the grate.

Long before it was done, Mr. Trelawney—you will remember that was the squire's name—had got up from his seat and was striding about the room. The doctor had taken off his powdered wig as if to hear better. He sat there, looking very strange indeed with his own close-cropped black hair.

At last, Mr. Dance finished the story.

"Mr. Dance," said the squire, "you are a very noble fellow. And as for riding down that black, dreadful villain, I regard it as an act of honor, sir. It was like stamping on a cockroach. This lad Hawkins is very dependable, I believe. Hawkins, will you ring that bell? Mr. Dance must have some ale."

"And so, Jim," said the doctor, "you have the thing

---

[1] A bust is a sculpture of the head, shoulders, and chest of a person.

that they were after, have you?"

"Here it is, sir," said I, and gave him the oilskin packet.

The doctor looked it all over, as if his fingers were itching to open it. But instead of doing that, he put it quietly in the pocket of his coat.

"Squire," said the doctor, "when Dance has had his ale he must, of course, be off on his Majesty's service. But I mean to keep Jim Hawkins here to sleep at my house. With your permission, I propose we should have the cold pie brought up and let him have supper."

"As you will, Livesey," said the squire. "Hawkins has earned better than cold pie."[2]

So a big pigeon pie was brought in and put on a side-table. I made a hearty supper, for I was as hungry as a hawk. Mr. Dance was further complimented and at last dismissed.

"And now, squire," said the doctor.

"And now, Livesey," said the squire, in the same breath.

"One at a time, one at a time," laughed Dr. Livesey. "You have heard of this Flint, I suppose?"

"Heard of him!" cried the squire. "Heard of him, you say! He was the most bloodthirsty buccaneer that sailed. Blackbeard[3] was a child next to Flint. I tell you, sir, the Spaniards were so terribly afraid of him that I was sometimes proud he was an Englishman. I've seen his top-sails with my own eyes off Trinidad. The cowardly son of a rum-puncheon[4] that I sailed with put back—put back, sir, into Port of Spain."[5]

"Well, I've heard of him myself in England," said the doctor. "But the point is, had he money?"

"Money!" cried the squire. "Have you heard the story? What were these villains after but money? What

[2] Pie, in this case, is a meat dish covered in pastry.
[3] Blackbeard (?-1718) was an English pirate known for his long, braided, black beard and for his ferociousness.
[4] A puncheon is an 84-gallon cask or barrel.
[5] Trinidad is an island in the West Indies. Port of Spain is the capital of Trinidad and Tobago, which make up a republic.

do they care for but money? What would they risk their rascal bodies for but money?"

"That we shall soon know," replied the doctor. "But you are so confounded hot-headed and excited that I cannot get a word in. What I want to know is this. Suppose that I have here in my pocket some clue to where Flint buried his treasure. Will that treasure amount to much?"

"Amount, sir!" cried the squire. "It will amount to this—if we have the clue you talk about, I'll equip a ship in Bristol dock. I'll take you and Hawkins here along. And I'll have that treasure if I search a year."

"Very well," said the doctor. "Now then, if Jim is agreeable, we'll open the packet."

He laid it before him on the table. The bundle was sewn together. The doctor had to get out his instrument case and cut the stitches with his medical scissors. It contained two things—a book and a sealed paper.

"First of all, we'll try the book," observed the doctor.

The squire and I were both peering over his shoulder as he opened it. Dr. Livesey had kindly motioned me to come round from the side table. I stopped eating to enjoy the sport of the search. On the first page there were only some scraps of writing, such as a man with a pen in his hand might make for boredom or practice. One was the same as the tattoo mark, "Billy Bones his fancy." Then there was "Mr. W. Bones, mate," "No more rum," and "Off Palm Key he got itt."

There were some other scratches, mostly **unintelligible** single words. I couldn't help wondering who it was that had "got itt," and what "itt" was that he got. A knife in his back as like as not.

"Not much instruction there," said Dr. Livesey, as he went on.

The next ten or twelve pages were filled with a strange series of entries. There was a date at one end of the line and at the other a sum of money, as in common account books. But instead of a written explanation, only a varying number of crosses were between the two.

For instance, on the 12th of June, 1745, a sum of seventy pounds had plainly become due to someone. But there was nothing but six crosses to explain the cause. To be sure, in a few cases the name of a place would be added, as "Offe Caraccas."[6] Or there would be a mere entry of latitude and longitude, as "62º 17' 20", 19º 2' 40"."[7]

The record lasted over nearly twenty years. The number of separate entries grew larger as time went on. At the end, a grand total had been made out after five or six wrong additions. These words were added: "Bones, his pile."

"I can't make head or tail of this," said Dr. Livesey.

"The thing is as clear as noonday," cried the squire. "This is the black-hearted hound's account book. These crosses stand for the names of ships or towns that they sank or **plundered**. The sums are the scoundrel's share. Where he feared an **ambiguity**, you see he added something clearer. 'Offe Caraccas,' for instance. You see, here was some unhappy vessel boarded off that coast. God help the poor souls that manned her—turned into coral[8] long ago."

"Right!" said the doctor. "See what it is to be a traveler. Right! And the amounts increase, you see, as he rose in rank."

There was little else in the volume but a few bearings of places noted in the blank pages towards the end. And there was a table for changing French, English, and Spanish moneys to a common value.

"Thrifty man!" cried the doctor. "He wasn't the one to be cheated."

"And now," said the squire, "for the other."

---

[6] Caracas is the capital of Venezuela, a country in South America.

[7] Latitude and longitude are read as degrees, minutes, and seconds. So the reading above would be 62 degrees, 17 minutes, 20 seconds; and 19 degrees, 2 minutes, and 40 seconds. A minute is a unit of measure equal to one-sixtieth of a degree. A second equals one-sixtieth of a minute.

[8] Coral is a hard substance formed by the skeletons of small sea animals.

The paper had been sealed in several places, using a thimble as a seal.[9] Perhaps it was the very thimble that I had found in the captain's pocket. The doctor opened the seals with great care and there fell out the map of an island. It showed the latitude and longitude, soundings, and names of hills and bays and inlets.[10] It had every detail that would be needed to bring a ship to a safe anchorage upon its shores.

The island was about nine miles long and five across. You might say it was shaped like a fat dragon standing up. It had two fine landlocked[11] harbors and a hill in the center marked "The Spy-glass."

There were several additions to the map made at a later date. Above all, there were three crosses of red ink—two on the north part of the island and one in the southwest. Beside this last were these words: "Bulk of treasure here." This was written in the same red ink and in a small neat hand. The writing was very different from the captain's shaky characters.

Over on the back the same hand had written this further information:

"*Tall tree, Spy-glass shoulder, bearing a point to the N. of N.N.E.*

Skeleton Island E.S.E. and by E.

Ten feet.

The bar silver is in the north **cache**. *You can find it in the direction of the east hill, ten fathoms south of the black cliff with the face on it.*

The arms are easy found, in the sand hill, N. point of north inlet cape, bearing E. and a quarter N.

J.F."

---

[9] Important documents were sealed with wax. While the wax was still warm, it was stamped, often with a ring. That way, the owner could tell if the seal had been broken. A thimble had been used to stamp the wax on the captain's papers.

[10] Bays are points where sea coasts curve inward. They are surrounded on three sides by land. Inlets are small streams or bays leading inland from larger bodies of water.

[11] *Landlocked* means "entirely or almost entirely surrounded by land."

That was all. But as brief and confusing as it was to me, it filled the squire and Dr. Livesey with delight.

"Livesey," said the squire, "you will give up this wretched practice at once. Tomorrow I start for Bristol. In three weeks' time—three weeks!—two weeks—ten days—we'll have the best ship, sir, and the finest crew in England.

"Hawkins shall come as cabin boy. You'll make a grand cabin boy, Hawkins. You, Livesey, are ship's doctor. I am admiral. We'll take Redruth, Joyce, and Hunter. We'll have favorable winds, a quick passage, and not the least difficulty in finding the spot. We'll have money to eat—to roll in—to play duck and drake with[12] ever after."

"Trelawney," said the doctor, "I'll go with you and I'll go bail[13] for it. So will Jim, and be a credit to the undertaking. There's only one man I'm afraid of."

"And who's that?" cried the squire. "Name the dog, sir!"

"You," replied the doctor, "for you cannot hold your tongue. We're not the only men who know of this paper. These fellows who attacked the inn tonight are bold, desperate men, for sure. Others stayed aboard that lugger. And I dare say there are more not far off. They are one and all, through thick and thin, bound that they'll get that money.

"We must none of us go alone till we get to sea," the doctor went on. "Jim and I shall stick together in the meanwhile. You'll take Joyce and Hunter when you ride to Bristol. From first to last, not one of us must breathe a word of what we've found."

"Livesey," replied the squire, "you are always in the right of it. I'll be as silent as the grave."

---

[12]Duck and drake is the game of skimming flat stones across the surface of calm water. It also means "to squander or throw away."
[13]*To go bail* for something means "willing to put up money or property as security."

PART II: THE SEA COOK

Chapter 7 (Summary)

I Go to Bristol

The doctor's plan of keeping Jim with him couldn't be carried out. Jim lived at Squire Trelawney's hall while the doctor went to London to find another doctor to take over his practice. The squire was away getting things ready for the sea journey. Jim spent his time studying the captain's map and dreaming of adventure. After a few weeks, a letter came from the squire, dated the first of March.

Squire Trelawney wrote that he had bought a two-hundred-ton schooner, the *Hispaniola*.[1] He said that everyone in Bristol had been very helpful since they heard about the treasure. Jim knew that the doctor would not be happy about that information getting out.

The squire went on to say that he at first had a hard time finding men for the crew—until a certain stroke of luck. A fine seaman named Long John Silver had just happened to be on the dock one day. Silver only had one leg. But he was an experienced sailor and would be their cook.

Silver had also been most helpful at finding other men for the crew. He had even gotten rid of two sailors already hired by the squire, saying they weren't suitable.

The squire had hired a captain, and Silver had found a mate named Arrow. The squire had also made arrangements for another ship to sail after them if they didn't return by the first of August. He suggested that before meeting him in Bristol, Jim should go and visit his

---

[1] A schooner is a sailing ship with two or more masts. The schooner had the advantage of speed and was able to go into shallow waters. The ship bought by Squire Trelawney was a three-masted schooner.

mother. He wrote that Jim should take the gamekeeper, Redruth, as a guard.

Jim was happy at the chance to visit home. He and Redruth went on foot to the "Admiral Benbow," where they found Jim's mother in good health. The squire had had the inn repaired and the sign repainted. He had even found a boy to work with Jim's mother while Jim was gone. Seeing the new boy made Jim realize that he really was leaving home. He shed a few tears.

The next day the mail stagecoach picked Jim and Redruth up and took them to Bristol. Jim was delighted with all the ships and the sailors with rings in their ears. Jim and Redruth found Squire Trelawney at an inn. He was dressed up like a sea officer and tried to walk like a sailor. The squire told them that the doctor had arrived and that they would sail the next day.

Chapter 8

At the Sign of the "Spy-glass"

Vocabulary Preview

The following words appear in this chapter. Review the list and get to know the words before you read the chapter.

anecdote—short story, usually about an amusing or interesting event
confidential—private; secret
dexterity—gracefulness; ease
mirth—happiness, often accompanied by laughter
sheepishly—with embarrassment; timidly

When I had finished breakfast, the squire gave me a note. It was addressed to John Silver at the "Spy-glass." The squire told me I should easily find the place by following the line of the docks. He said to keep a bright lookout for a little tavern with a large brass telescope for a sign.

I set off, overjoyed at this opportunity to see some more of the ships and seamen. The dock was now at its busiest. I picked my way among a great crowd of people and carts and bundles of goods until I found the tavern in question.

It was a bright enough little place of entertainment. The sign was newly painted and the windows had neat red curtains. The floor was cleanly sanded. There was a street on either side and an open door on both. The doors made the large, low room pretty clear to see in, in spite of clouds of tobacco smoke.

The customers were mostly seafaring men. They talked so loudly that I hung at the door, almost afraid to enter.

As I was waiting, a man came out of a side room. At a glance, I was sure he must be Long John. His left leg was cut off close by the hip. Under the left shoulder he carried a crutch which he managed with wonderful **dexterity**. He hopped about upon it like a bird.

Long John was very tall and strong. His face was as big as a ham—plain and pale but intelligent and smiling. Indeed, he seemed in the most cheerful spirits. He whistled as he moved about among the tables with a merry word or a slap on the shoulder for the more favored of his guests.

Now, to tell you the truth, from the very first mention of Long John in Squire Trelawney's letter, I had taken a fear in my mind. I was afraid that he might prove to be the very one-legged sailor I had watched for so long at the old "Benbow."

But one look at the man before me was enough. I had seen the captain and Black Dog and the blind man Pew. I thought I knew what a buccaneer was like. It was a very different creature—according to me—from this clean and pleasant-tempered landlord.

I plucked up courage at once and crossed the entryway. I walked right up to the man where he stood, propped on his crutch, talking to a customer.

"Mr. Silver, sir?" I asked, holding out the note.

"Yes, my lad," said he. "Such is my name, to be sure. And who may you be?"

And then he saw the squire's letter. He seemed to me to give something almost like a jump of surprise.

"Oh!" said he, quite loud, and offering his hand. "I see. You are our new cabin boy. Pleased I am to see you."

And he took my hand in his large, firm grasp.

Just then one of the customers at the far side rose

suddenly and made for the door. It was close by him, and he was out in the street in a moment. But his hurry had attracted my notice and I recognized him at a glance. It was the waxy-faced man missing two fingers—the one who had come first to the "Admiral Benbow."

"Oh," I cried, "stop him! It's Black Dog!"

"I don't care two coppers who he is," cried Silver. "But he hasn't paid his bill. Harry, run and catch him."

One of the others who was nearest the door leaped up and started in pursuit.

"If he were Admiral Hawke,[1] he shall pay his bill," cried Silver. Then, releasing my hand, he asked, "Who did you say he was? Black what?"

"Dog, sir," said I. "Hasn't Mr. Trelawney told you of the buccaneers? He was one of them."

"So?" cried Silver. "In my house! Ben, run and help Harry. One of those swabs, was he? Was that you drinking with him, Morgan? Step up here."

The man whom he called Morgan was an old, gray-haired sailor with a reddish-brown face. He came forward pretty **sheepishly,** rolling his quid.[2]

"Now, Morgan," said Long John, very sternly. "You never clapped your eyes on that Black—Black Dog before, did you now?"

"Not I, sir," said Morgan, with a salute.

"You didn't know his name, did you?"

"No, sir."

"By the powers, Tom Morgan, that's good for you!" exclaimed the landlord. "If you had been mixed up with the like of that, you would never have put another foot in my house. You may lay to that. And what was he saying to you?"

"I don't rightly know, sir," answered Morgan.

"Do you call that a head on your shoulders or a blessed dead eye?" cried Long John. "Don't rightly know, don't you! Perhaps you don't happen to rightly know who

---

[1] Edward Hawke was a famous British admiral in the 18th century.
[2] A quid is a chunk of something chewable. The sailors chewed tobacco.

you was speaking to, perhaps? Come now, what was he talking about—voyages, cap'ns, ships? Pipe up! What was it?"

"We was a-talkin' of keel-hauling," answered Morgan.

"Keel-hauling, was you? And a mighty suitable thing, too, and you may lay to that. Get back to your place for a lubber, Tom."

Morgan rolled back to his seat. Then Silver said to me in a **confidential** whisper that was very flattering, as I thought:

"He's quite an honest man, Tom Morgan. Only stupid. And now," he ran on again aloud, "let's see— Black Dog? No, I don't know the name, not I. Yet I kind of think I've—yes, I've seen the swab. He used to come here with a blind beggar, he did."

"That he did, you may be sure," said I. "I knew that blind man, too. His name was Pew."

"It was!" cried Silver, now quite excited. "Pew! That were his name for certain. Ah, he looked like a shark, he did! If we run down this Black Dog, now, there'll be news for Cap'n Trelawney! Ben's a good runner. Few seamen run better than Ben. He should run him down, hand over hand,[3] by the powers! He talked o' keel-hauling, did he? *I'll* keel-haul him!"

All the time he was jerking out these phrases, he was stumping up and down the tavern on the crutch. He kept slapping tables with his hand. He gave a show of excitement that would have convinced an Old Bailey judge or a Bow Street runner.[4]

My suspicions had been thoroughly awakened again on finding Black Dog at the "Spy-glass." I watched Silver closely, but he was too deep and too ready and too clever for me.

---

[3] "In this case, *hand over hand* means "to overtake someone very quickly." It comes from the hand-over-hand motion of climbing or hauling in a rope.

[4] Old Bailey is the Central Criminal Court in London. Bow Street runners were the first police and detective force in England. They were organized in the mid-18th century.

The two men came back out of breath and confessed that they had lost the track in a crowd. Long John scolded them like thieves. By the time all this occurred, I would have sworn on the innocence of Long John Silver.

"See here now, Hawkins," said Silver. "Here's a blessed hard thing on a man like me, now, ain't it? There's Cap'n Trelawney—what's he to think? Here I have this confounded son of a Dutchman sitting in my own house, drinking of my own rum! Here you comes and tells me of it plain. And here I let him give us all the slip before my blessed deadlights!

"Now, Hawkins," Silver went on, "you do me justice with the cap'n. You're a lad, you are, but you're as smart as paint. I see that when you first came in. Now, here it is. What could I do with this old timber I hobble on? When I was a master mariner,[5] I'd have come up alongside of him, hand over hand. I'd have broached him to in a brace of old shakes,[6] I would. But now—"

And then, all of a sudden, he stopped. His jaw dropped as though he had remembered something.

"The bill!" he burst out. "Three goes o' rum! Why shiver my timbers, if I hadn't forgotten my bill!"

And, falling on a bench, he laughed until the tears ran down his cheeks. I couldn't help joining. We laughed together, peal after peal, until the tavern rang again.

"Why, what a precious old sea-calf I am!" he said at last, wiping his cheeks. "You and me should get on well, Hawkins, for I'll take my davy[7] I should be rated ship's boy. But come now, stand by to go about.[8] This won't do. Duty is duty, mates. I'll put on my old cocked hat and step along with you to Cap'n Trelawney and report this here affair. For, mind you, it's serious, young Hawkins. Neither you nor me's come out of it with what I should so

---

[5] A master mariner is a high-ranking sailor.
[6] *Broached* means "to veer sideways across the waves," therefore to be in danger of capsizing. *In a brace of old shakes* means "as soon as you can shake the dice-box twice," or "instantly."
[7] *Davy* means "affidavit," a written statement made under an oath of honesty.
[8] *To go about* or *to come about* means "to turn the ship."

boldly call credit. Nor you neither, says you. Not smart—none of the pair of us is smart. But dash my buttons! That was a good 'un about my bill."

And he began to laugh heartily again. I didn't see the joke as he did. But I was again obliged to join him in his **mirth**.

On our little walk along the quays, he made himself the most interesting companion. He told me about the different ships that we passed—their rig, tonnage, and nationality. He explained the work that was going on—how one was unloading, another taking in cargo, and a third getting ready for sea. Every now and then he told me some little **anecdote** of ships or seamen. Or he repeated a nautical phrase till I had learned it perfectly. I began to see that here was one of the best possible shipmates.

When we got to the inn, the squire and Dr. Livesey were seated together. They were finishing a quart of ale with a toast in it[9] before they should go aboard the schooner on a visit of inspection.

Long John told the story from first to last. He spoke with a great deal of spirit and the most perfect truth. "That was how it were, now, weren't it, Hawkins?" he would say now and again. I could always back him up completely.

The two gentlemen regretted that Black Dog had got away. But we all agreed there was nothing to be done. After he had been complimented, Long John took up his crutch and departed.

"All hands aboard by four this afternoon," shouted the squire after him.

"Aye, aye, sir," cried the cook from the hallway.

"Well, squire," said Dr. Livesey, "I don't put much faith in your discoveries as a general thing. But I will say this, John Silver suits me."

"The man's a perfect trump,"[10] declared the squire.

---

[9] Drinks were sometimes flavored with pieces of spiced toast.
[10] A trump is a dependable and responsible person.

"And now," added the doctor, "Jim may come on board with us, may he not?"

"To be sure he may," said squire. "Take your hat, Hawkins, and we'll see the ship."

Chapter 9 (Summary)

Powder and Arms

Jim Hawkins, Squire Trelawney, and Dr. Livesey all went out to the *Hispaniola* in a small boat. When they stepped aboard, they were greeted by Mr. Arrow, the new mate. Arrow was a tanned old sailor, with earrings in his ear and a squint. He was very friendly with the squire.

Captain Smollett, an angry-looking man, was very different from Arrow. He grimly expressed his dislike of the men and the cruise. The squire was annoyed, but Dr. Livesey calmly asked the captain to explain why he was upset.

Smollett replied that he disliked the crew and thought he should have been able to choose his own men. He felt that Mr. Arrow was too friendly with the crew to be a good officer.

The captain said he had heard from his hands that they were going after treasure. Smollett didn't like treasure voyages. Smollett also was displeased because the men knew more about the voyage than he did and they supposedly had seen the treasure map. The men claimed to know the latitude and longitude of the treasure's location.

The squire seemed surprised that the crew knew so much about the map. But neither he nor the doctor seemed too worried about it.

Smollett insisted that the squire and Dr. Livesey take certain actions. Smollett told them to store the powder and the weapons under the cabin. He also said they should keep their own people bunked together near the cabin. And he warned them to keep the treasure map hidden.

If these orders weren't followed, Smollett threatened to leave the ship. The doctor noticed the captain's fears that the hired sailors weren't trustworthy. The squire unwillingly agreed that things would be rearranged as Smollett asked. With that, the captain left.

Dr. Livesey told the squire that he had at least two honest men on the ship—Captain Smollett and Long John Silver. The squire said that he liked Silver, but not the captain.

While the men were moving the powder, Silver came on board. The cook complained that the delay of moving everything about would cause them to miss the tide. However, Captain Smollett was firm. He sent Silver below and soon sent Jim down to help the cook. Jim overheard Captain Smollett say to the doctor that he wouldn't play favorites on the ship. Jim decided that he really hated the captain.

Chapter 10 (Summary)

The Voyage

Everyone worked all night getting ready for the voyage. In the morning, Jim was exhausted, but he was too excited to leave the deck. As the crew turned the capstan bars to raise the anchor, they sang: "Fifteen men on the dead man's chest—Yo-ho-ho, and a bottle of rum!"

At the beginning, the voyage was not difficult. The ship was solid, the crew was capable, and the captain knew his business. But the mate, Mr. Arrow, began to appear on deck drunk. He had no authority over the men and was useless as an officer. One dark night, Arrow disappeared. Apparently he had fallen overboard.

Long John Silver was the man the crew most respected. When he gave orders they obeyed him without any resentment. Because he was the cook, the sailors called him Barbecue. Silver got around deck very well, even with his wooden leg.

Silver had a parrot he had named Captain Flint, after the famous pirate. The bird would yell "Pieces of eight! Pieces of eight!"[1] over and over again. It also swore loudly. Silver said the old bird had seen as much evil as the devil.

The squire and captain were still not getting along very well. However, Captain Smollett did admit that the crew seemed to be trustworthy. But he felt the squire spoiled the hands by having birthday celebrations and leaving an apple barrel open for anybody who was hungry. Smollett felt that no good would come of a spoiled crew.

But some good did come of the open apple barrel.

---

[1] Pieces of eight were silver Spanish coins. They were often cut into pieces to make change.

The evening before they expected to sight Treasure Island—as they called it—Jim decided to get an apple. He went on deck and got into the barrel, searching for the few apples left in the bottom.

Sitting in the barrel, Jim was relaxed by the ship's motion and the sounds of the water. He had just about fallen asleep when someone sat down next to the apple barrel. Just as Jim was about to jump up and reveal himself, the man began to speak. It was Long John Silver.

When Jim heard Silver's first words, he lay there trembling. Now Jim knew that the lives of the honest men on the ship depended on him alone.

Chapter 11

What I Heard in the Apple Barrel

Vocabulary Preview

The following words appear in this chapter. Review the list and get to know the words before you read the chapter.

audible—clear; able to be heard
derisively—insultingly; in a nasty tone
marooned—deserted; left behind
rogue—scoundrel; villain

N o, not I," said Silver. "Flint was cap'n. I was quartermaster, with my timber leg. The same broadside I lost my leg, old Pew lost his eyes. It was a master surgeon that took my leg off. He was out of college and all—Latin by the bucket and what not. But he was hanged like a dog and sun-dried like the rest at Corso Castle.[1]

"That was Roberts' men, that was," Silver went on. "It all comed of changing the names of their ships—*Royal Fortune* and so on. Now what a ship was christened, let her stay, I says. So it was with the *Cassandra*. She brought us all safe home from Malabar[2] after England took the *Viceroy of the Indies*. So it was with the old *Walrus*, Flint's old ship. I've seen that one a-muck with the red blood

---

[1] Corso Castle was a British port on the west coast of Africa where Africans were bought for the slave trade. The scaffolds were in plain view to the traffic on the river. Bodies of hanged criminals were sometimes caged and left in the sun. Sometimes the bodies were tarred to preserve them so they could be viewed for a long time.
[2] Malabar is a coastal area in southwest India.

and fit to sink with gold."

"Ah!" cried another. It was the voice of the youngest hand on board and sounded full of admiration. "He was the flower of the flock, was Flint!"

"Davis[3] was a man, too, by all accounts," said Silver. "I never sailed alongside of him. First with England, then with Flint, that's my story.[4] And now here on my own account, in a manner of speaking. I laid by nine hundred pounds[5] safe from England and two thousand after Flint. That ain't bad for a man before the mast[6]—all safe in the bank.

"'Tain't earning now, it's saving does it, you may bet on that," continued the cook. "Where's all England's men now? I dunno. Where's Flint's? Why most of 'em aboard here and glad to get the food. Been begging before that, some of 'em.

"Old Pew, who had lost his sight and might have thought shame, spends twelve hundred pounds in a year like a lord in Parliament. Where is he now? Well, he's dead now and buried. But for two year before that, shiver my timbers! The man was starving. He begged and he stole and he cut throats. And he starved at that, by the powers!"

"Well, it ain't much use, after all," said the young seaman.

"'Tain't much use for fools, you may bet on it—that nor nothing," cried Silver. "But now, you look here. You're young, you are, but you're as smart as paint. I see that when I set my eyes on you. I'll talk to you like a man."

You may imagine how I felt when I heard this. The disgusting old **rogue** was addressing another in the very

---

[3] Captain Howell Davis was a famous pirate in the early 1700s.

[4] Some pirates first served in the English navy. In other cases, pirates offered their services to countries at war. They were then called "privateers" and they limited their raids to the ships of the enemy countries. After their service ended, many privateers turned to piracy. The term "buccaneer" originally referred to a privateer.

[5] A pound is a unit of money in England and other countries.

[6] A sailor "before the mast" is one of the lowest-ranked sailors.

same words of flattery he had used on me. If I had been able, I think I would have killed him through the barrel. Meantime, Silver ran on, little supposing he was overheard.

"Here it is about gentlemen of fortune. They lives rough and they risk hanging. But they eat and drink like fighting-cocks.[7] And when a cruise is done—why, it's hundreds of pounds instead of hundreds of farthings in their pockets.[8] Now the most goes for rum and a good fling. Then they put to sea again in their shirts.

"But that's not the course I lay," Silver went on. "I puts it all away, some here, some there, and none too much anywheres. That way I don't rouse suspicion. I'm fifty, mark you. Once back from this cruise, I set up as a gentleman in earnest. Time enough, too, says you. Ah, but I've lived easy in the meantime. I never denied myself o' nothing my heart desires. I've slept soft and ate dainty all my days, except when at sea. And how did I begin? Before the mast, like you!"

"Well," said the other, "but all the other money's gone now, ain't it? You don't dare show face in Bristol after this voyage."

"Why, where might you suppose it was?" asked Silver, **derisively**.

"At Bristol, in banks and places," answered his companion.

"It were," said the cook. "It were when we weighed anchor. But my old missis has it all by now. And the "Spy-glass" is sold, lease and goodwill and rigging.[9] And the old girl's off to meet me. I would tell you where, for I trust you, but it'd make jealousy among the mates."

"And can you trust your missis?" asked the other.

"Gentlemen of fortune," replied the cook, "usually trust little among themselves. And right they are, you may lay to it. But I have a way with me, I have. There was

[7] Fighting-cocks are roosters trained to fight other roosters in contest.
[8] A farthing was worth one-fourth of a penny. It was practically worthless.
[9] In this case, "rigging" refers to all the things needed to run the inn.

some that was feared of Pew and some that was feared of Flint. But Flint his own self was feared of me. Feared he was, and proud.

"They was the roughest crew afloat, was Flint's," continued Silver. "The devil himself would have been feared to go to sea with them. Well now, I tell you, I'm not a boasting man, and you can see how easy I keep company. But when I was quartermaster, *lambs* wasn't the word for Flint's old buccaneers. Ah, you may be sure of yourself in John's ship."

"Well, I tell you now," replied the lad, "I didn't half a quarter like the job till I had this talk with you, John. But there's my hand on it now."

"And a brave lad you were, and smart, too," answered Silver. They shook hands so heartily that the barrel shook. "And a finer figurehead for a gentleman of fortune I never clapped my eyes on."

By this time I had begun to understand the meaning of their terms. By a "gentleman of fortune" they plainly meant neither more nor less than a common pirate. The little scene that I had overheard was the last act in the corruption of one of the honest hands—perhaps of the last one left aboard.

But on this point I was soon to be relieved. Silver gave a little whistle and a third man strolled up and sat down by the party.

"Dick's square," said Silver, referring to the young lad.

"Oh, I know'd Dick was square," replied the voice of the coxswain, Israel Hands.[10] "He's no fool, is Dick." And he turned his quid and spat. "But look here," he went on. "Here's what I want to know, Barbecue. How long are we a-going to stand off and on like a blessed bumboat? I've had almost enough of Cap'n Smollett. He's hazed[11] me long enough, by thunder! I want to go into that cabin, I

[10]Stevenson took the name "Israel Hands" from that of an actual pirate who sailed with the famous Blackbeard.

[11]To haze is to harass someone by making him or her perform difficult or disagreeable work.

do. I want their pickles and wines and that."

"Israel," said Silver, "your head ain't much account, nor ever was. But you're able to hear, I reckon. At least, your ears is big enough. Now here's what I say: you'll bunk forward and you'll live hard and you'll speak soft and you'll keep sober till I give the word. And you may lay to that, my son."

"Well, I don't say no, do I?" growled the coxswain. "What I say is, when? That's what I say."

"When! By the powers!" cried Silver. "Well now, if you want to know, I'll tell you when. The last moment I can manage, and that's when. Here's a first-rate seaman, Cap'n Smollett, sails the blessed ship for us. Here's this squire and doctor with a map and such—I don't know where it is, do I? No more do you, says you. Well, then, I mean this squire and doctor shall find the stuff and help us to get it aboard, by the powers. Then we'll see. If I was sure of you all, sons of double Dutchmen, I'd have Cap'n Smollett navigate us halfway back again before I struck."

"Why, we're all seamen aboard here, I should think," said the lad Dick.

"We're all forecastle hands, you mean," snapped Silver. "We can steer a course, but who's to set one? That's what all you gentlemen split on, first and last. If I had my way, I'd have Cap'n Smollett work us back into the trade winds at least. Then we'd have no blessed miscalculations and a spoonful of water a day.

"But I know the sort you are," Silver continued. "I'll finish with 'em at the island, as soon's the stuff's on board, and a pity it is. But you're never happy till you're drunk. Split my sides, I've a sick heart to sail with the likes of you!"

"Easy all, Long John," cried Israel. "Who's a-crossin' you?"

"Why, think ye now, how many tall ships have I seen boarded? And how many brisk lads drying in the sun at Execution Dock?"[12] cried Silver. "And all for this same

[12]Execution Dock was at Wapping, on the Thames River.

hurry and hurry and hurry. You hear me? I seen a thing or two at sea, I have. If you would only lay your course and a point to windward, you would ride in carriages, you would. But not you! I know you. You'll have your mouthful of rum tomorrow and go hang."

"Everybody know'd you was a kind of a chaplain,[13] John. But there's others who could hand and steer as well as you," said Israel. "They liked a bit o' fun, they did. They wasn't so high and dry, nohow. Everyone took their fling like jolly companions."

"So?" says Silver. "Well, and where are they now? Pew was that sort and he died a beggarman. Flint was, and he died of rum at Savannah. Ah, they was a sweet crew, they was! Only, where are they?"

"But," asked Dick, "when we do cross them, what are we to do with 'em, anyhow?"

"There's the man for me!" cried the cook, with admiration. "That's what I call business. Well, what would you think? Put 'em ashore, **marooned?** That would have been England's way. Or cut 'em down like that much pork? That would have been Flint's or Billy Bones' way."

"Billy was the man for that," said Israel. " 'Dead men don't bite,' says he. Well, he's dead now hisself. He knows the long and short of it now. And if ever a rough hand come to port, it was Billy."

"Right you are," said Silver. "Rough and ready. But mark you here: I'm an easy man—I'm quite the gentleman, says you. But this time it's serious. Duty is duty, mates. I give my vote—death. One day I'll be in Parlment[14] and riding in my coach. I don't want none of these sea-lawyers in the cabin a-coming home unlooked for like the devil at prayers. Wait is what I say. But when the time comes, why, let her rip!"

"John," cried the coxswain, "you're a man!"

"You'll say so, Israel, when you see," said Silver.

---

[13]A chaplain is a minister who usually serves in the armed forces or in places such as hospitals and prisons.

[14]Parliament is made up of elected officials who make laws in England.

"Only one thing I claim—I claim Trelawney. I'll wring his calf's head off his body with these hands. Dick!" he added, breaking off. "You just jump up, like a sweet lad, and get me an apple to wet my pipe like."

You may fancy the terror I was in! I would have leaped out and run for it, if I had found the strength. But my limbs and heart alike let me down. I heard Dick begin to rise, and then it seemed someone stopped him.

The voice of Hands exclaimed, "Oh, stow that! Don't you go swallowing that bilge, John. Let's have a go of the rum."

"Dick," said Silver, "I trust you. I've marked the keg, mind you. There's the key. You fill a cup and bring it up."

Terrified as I was, I couldn't help thinking about Mr. Arrow. This must have been how he got the strong waters that destroyed him.

Dick was gone but a little while. During his absence, Israel spoke straight on in the cook's ear. It was only a word or two that I could catch. Yet I gathered some important news. Besides other scraps that tended to the same purpose, one whole clause was **audible:** "Not another man of them'll join." So there were still faithful men on board.

When Dick returned, one after another of the trio took the cup and drank—one "to luck," another with a "Here's to old Flint." Silver himself said in a kind of song, "Here's to ourselves, and hold your luff, plenty of prizes and plenty of duff."

Just then a sort of brightness fell upon me in the barrel. Looking up, I found the moon had risen. It was silvering the mizzen-top and shining white on the luff of the foresail. Almost at the same time the voice of the lookout shouted, "Land-ho!"

Chapter 12

Council of War[1]

There was a great rush of feet across the deck. I could hear people tumbling up from the cabin and the forecastle. Slipping in an instant outside my barrel, I dived behind the foresail and doubled back towards the stern. I came out upon the open deck in time to join Hunter and Dr. Livesey in the rush for the weather bow.

There, all hands were already gathered. A belt of fog had lifted almost with the appearance of the moon. Away to the southwest of us we saw two low hills, about a couple of miles apart. Rising behind one of them was a third and higher hill, whose peak was still buried in the fog. All three seemed sharp and cone-shaped.

So much I saw, almost in a dream. For I hadn't yet recovered from my horrid fear of a minute or two before. And then I heard the voice of Captain Smollett issuing orders. The *Hispaniola* was laid a couple of points nearer the wind. She now sailed a course that would just clear

---

[1] A council of war is a meeting in which top officers plan their strategy.

the island on the east.

"And now, men," said the captain, when all was sheeted home.[2] "Has any one of you ever seen that land ahead?"

"I have, sir," said Silver. "I've watered there with a trader I was cook in."

"The anchorage[3] is on the south, behind an island, I fancy?" asked the captain.

"Yes, sir. Skeleton Island, they calls it. It were a main place for pirates once. A hand we had on board knowed all their names for it. That hill to the northward they calls Foremast Hill. There are three hills in a row running southward. But the main—that's the big 'un with the cloud on it—they usually call the Spy-glass. That was because of a lookout they kept when they was in the anchorage, cleaning. For it's there they cleaned their ships, sir, asking your pardon."

"I have a chart here," said Captain Smollett. "See if that's the place."

Long John's eyes burned in his head as he took the chart. But, by the fresh look of the paper, I knew he was doomed to disappointment. This was not the map we found in Billy Bones' chest, but an accurate copy. It was complete in all things—names and heights and soundings—with the single exception of the red crosses and the written notes. Silver's annoyance must have been sharp. But he had the strength of mind to hide it.

"Yes, sir," said Silver, "this is the spot to be sure, and very prettily drawn out. Who might have done that, I wonder? The pirates were too ignorant, I reckon. Ay, here it is: 'Captain Kidd's Anchorage'[4]—just the name my shipmate called it. There's a strong current that runs along the south and then away northward up the west

---

[2] The sails are sheeted home when they have been set as flat (vertical) as possible. This is done by pulling on the lines, called sheets, that control the angle of the sails.

[3] An anchorage is a place for a ship to drop its anchor.

[4] Captain Kidd was a famous British privateer and pirate. He was hanged in 1701.

coast. Right you was, sir," said he, "to haul your wind and keep the weather of the island. At least, if that was your intention to enter and careen. And there ain't no better place for that in these waters."

"Thank you, my man," said Captain Smollett. "I'll ask you later on to give us a help. You may go."

I was surprised at the coolness with which John **avowed** his knowledge of the island. I own I was half frightened when I saw him drawing nearer to me. He didn't know, to be sure, that I had overheard his meeting from the apple barrel. Yet by this time I had taken a horror of his cruelty, disloyalty, and power. I could barely hide a shudder when he laid his hand upon my arm.

"Ah," said he, "this here is a sweet spot, this island. It's a sweet spot for a lad to get ashore on. You'll bathe and you'll climb trees and you'll hunt goats, you will. You'll get aloft on them hills like a goat yourself.

"Why, it makes me young again," he went on. "I was going to forget my timber leg, I was. It's a pleasant thing to be young and have ten toes. You may lay to that. When you want to go on a bit of exploring, you just ask old John. He'll put up a snack for you to take along."

He clapped me in the friendliest way on the shoulder. Then he hobbled off forward and went below.

Captain Smollett, the squire, and Dr. Livesey were talking together on the quarterdeck. I was anxious to tell them my story. But I didn't dare interrupt them openly. While I was still casting about in my thoughts to find some probable excuse, Dr. Livesey called me to his side. He had left his pipe below. Being a slave to tobacco, he had meant that I should fetch it. But as soon as I was near enough to speak and not be overheard, I broke out immediately.

"Doctor, let me speak. Get the captain and squire down to the cabin. Then make some excuse to send for me. I have terrible news."

The doctor changed his expression a little, but the next moment he was master of himself.

"Thank you, Jim," said he, quite loudly. "That was all I wanted to know." He spoke as though he had asked me a question.

And with that, he turned on his heel and rejoined the other two. They spoke together for a little. None of them started or raised his voice or so much as whistled. However, it was plain enough that Dr. Livesey had communicated my request. The next thing that I heard was the captain giving an order to Job Anderson, the boatswain, and all hands were piped on deck.

"My lads," said Captain Smollett to the crew, "I've a word to say to you. This land that we've sighted is the place we've been sailing to. Mr. Trelawney—being a very open-handed gentleman, as we all know—has just asked me a word or two. I was able to tell him that every man on board had done his duty, below and aloft. I never ask to see it done better. So he and I and the doctor are going below to the cabin to drink to *your* health and luck. You'll have grog served out for you to drink to *our* health and luck. I'll tell you what I think of this: I think it handsome. And if you think as I do, you'll give a good sea cheer for the gentleman that does it."

The cheer followed—that was a matter of course. But it rang out so full and hearty, I confess I could hardly believe these same men were plotting for our blood.

"One more cheer for Cap'n Smollett," cried Long John, when the first had **subsided.**

And this also was given with a will.

On the top of that, the three gentlemen went below. Not long after, word was sent forward that Jim Hawkins was wanted in the cabin.

I found them all three seated round the table, a bottle of Spanish wine and some raisins before them. The doctor was smoking away, with his wig on his lap. That, I knew, was a sign that he was **agitated.** The stern window was open, for it was a warm night. You could see the moon shining behind on the ship's wake.

"Now, Hawkins," said the squire, "you have

something to say. Speak up."

I did as I was bid. As short as I could make it, I told the whole details of Silver's conversation. Nobody interrupted me till I was done. Nor did any one of the three of them make so much as a movement. They kept their eyes upon my face from first to last.

"Jim," said Dr. Livesey, "take a seat."

And they made me sit down at the table beside them. They poured me out a glass of wine and filled my hands with raisins. All three—one after the other and each with a bow—drank to my good health and their service to me for my luck and courage.

"Now, captain," said the squire, "you were right and I was wrong. I admit I'm an ass and I await your orders."

"No more an ass than I, sir," replied the captain. "I never heard of a crew that meant to **mutiny** who didn't show signs before. Then any man that had an eye in his head could see the mischief and take steps according. But this crew," he added, "beats me."

"Captain," said the doctor, "with your permission, that's Silver. A very remarkable man."

"He'd look remarkably well hanging from a yard-arm, sir," replied the captain. "But this is talk. This don't lead to anything. I see three or four points. With Mr. Trelawney's permission, I'll name them."

"You, sir, are the captain. It is for you to speak," said Mr. Trelawney, grandly.

"First point," began Mr. Smollett. "We must go on because we can't turn back. If I gave the word to go about, they would rise at once. Second point, we have time before us—at least until this treasure's found. Third point, there are faithful hands.

"Now, sir," continued the captain, "it's got to come to blows sooner or later. What I propose is to take time by the forelock,[5] as the saying is, and come to blows some fine day when they least expect it. I take it we can count on your own home servants, Mr. Trelawney?"

---

[5] A forelock is a clump of hair that falls across the forehead.

"As upon myself," declared the squire.

"Three," reckoned the captain. "Ourselves makes seven, counting Hawkins, here. Now, about the honest hands?"

"Most likely Trelawney's own men," said the doctor. "Those he had picked up for himself before he lit on Silver."

"No," replied the squire. "Israel Hands was one of mine."

"I did think I could have trusted Hands," added the captain.

"And to think that they're all Englishmen!" broke out the squire. "Sir, I could find it in my heart to blow the ship up."

"Well, gentlemen," said the captain, "the best that I can say is not much. We must lay to and keep a bright lookout, if you please. It's hard on a man, I know. It would be more pleasant to come to blows. But there's no help for it till we know our men. Lay to and whistle for a wind, that's my view."

"Jim here," said the doctor, "can help us more than anyone. The men are not shy with him, and Jim is a noticing lad."

"Hawkins, I put tremendous faith in you," added the squire.

I began to feel pretty desperate at this, for I felt altogether helpless. Yet—by an odd train of events—it was indeed through me that safety came. In the meantime, talk as we pleased, there were only seven out of the twenty-six on whom we knew we could rely. And out of those seven, one was a boy. So the grown men on our side were six to their nineteen.

PART III: MY SHORE ADVENTURE

Chapter 13

How I Began My Shore Adventure

Vocabulary Preview

The following words appear in this chapter. Review the list and get to know the words before you read the chapter.

civility—courtesy; respect
embark—set out; get underway
grudgingly—unwillingly
melancholy—gloomy; cheerless
pedestal—stand; platform used to display a treasured object
stagnant—foul; stale

When I came on deck next morning, the appearance of the island was altogether changed. Although the breeze had now utterly failed, we had made a great deal of way during the night. We were now lying becalmed about half a mile to the southeast of the low eastern coast.

Gray-colored woods covered a large part of the surface. Indeed, this even tint was broken up by streaks of yellow sand in the lower lands. Many tall trees of the pine family out-topped the others—some singly, some in clumps. But the general coloring was uniform and sad.

The hills ran up clear above the vegetation in blades of naked rock. All were strangely shaped. The Spyglass—which was by three or four hundred feet the tallest on the island—was likewise the strangest in shape. It ran straight up from almost every side, then suddenly cut off at the top like a **pedestal** to put a statue on.

The *Hispaniola* was rolling scuppers under in the ocean swell. The booms were tearing at the blocks. The rudder was banging to and fro. And the whole ship was creaking, groaning, and jumping like a factory.

I had to cling tight to the back stay, and the world turned dizzily before my eyes. I was a good enough sailor when we were up and going. But this standing still and being rolled about like a bottle was a thing I never learned to stand without a qualm or so—especially in the morning on an empty stomach.

Perhaps it was this that made my heart sink into my boots, as the saying is. Or perhaps it was the look of the island with its gray, **melancholy** woods and wild stone spires.[1] Maybe it was the surf that we could both see and hear foaming and thundering on the steep beach.

The sun shone bright and hot, and the shore birds were fishing and crying all around us. And you would have thought anyone would have been glad to get to land after being so long at sea. But from that first look, I hated the very thought of Treasure Island.

We had a dreary morning's work before us, for there was no sign of any wind. The boats had to be got out and manned. The ship had to be pulled three or four miles round the corner of the island and up the narrow passage to the anchorage behind Skeleton Island.

I volunteered for one of the boats, where I had no business, of course. The heat was sweltering and the men grumbled fiercely over their work. Anderson, the boatswain, was in command of my boat. He had also taken over duties of first mate after Arrow had disappeared. But now, instead of keeping the crew in order, he grumbled as loud as the worst.

"Well," Anderson said, with an oath, "it's not forever."

---

[1] Spires are top parts of pointed objects.

I thought this was a very bad sign. Up to that day, the men had gone briskly and willingly about their business. But the very sight of the island had relaxed the cords of discipline.

All the way in, Long John stood by the steersman and directed the ship. He knew the passage like the palm of his hand. Though the man in the chains measured everywhere more water than was down in the chart, John never hesitated once.

"There's a strong scour with the ebb,"[2] he said. "And this here passage has been dug out with a spade, in a manner of speaking."

We brought up just where the anchor was in the chart. We were about a third of a mile from either shore. The mainland was on one side and Skeleton Island on the other. The bottom was clean sand. The plunge of our anchor sent up clouds of birds wheeling and crying over the woods. But in less than a minute they were down again, and all was once more silent.

The place was entirely surrounded by land. It was buried in woods, the trees coming right down to high-water mark. The shores were mostly flat. The hilltops stood round at a distance in a sort of amphitheater,[3] one here, one there.

Two little rivers—or rather, two swamps—emptied out into this pond, as you might call it. The growth around that part of the shore had a kind of blinding brightness. From the ship, we could see nothing of the house or stockade,[4] for they were quite buried among trees. If it hadn't been for the chart on the companion, we might have been the first that had ever anchored there since the island arose out of the sea.

There wasn't a breath of air moving. There wasn't a sound but that of the surf booming half a mile away along the beaches and against the rocks outside. A strange

[2] The ebb is the time when the tide is going out.
[3] An amphitheater is an oval or round structure with rows of seats rising around an open central area.
[4] A stockade is a fence used for defensive purposes.

stagnant smell hung over the anchorage—a smell of sodden leaves and rotted tree trunks. I observed the doctor sniffing and sniffing, like someone tasting a bad egg.

"I don't know about treasure," he said, "but I'll stake my wig there's fever here."

The behavior of the men had been alarming in the boat. But it became truly threatening when they had come aboard. They lay about the deck growling together in talk. The slightest order was received with a black look and **grudgingly** and carelessly obeyed. Even the honest hands must have caught the infection, for there was not one man aboard to mend another. It was plain that mutiny hung over us like a thundercloud.

And it wasn't only we of the cabin party who felt the danger. Long John was hard at work going from group to group, spending himself in good advice. No man could have shown a better example. He fairly outdid himself in willingness and **civility.** He was all smiles to everyone.

If an order were given, John would be on his crutch in an instant with the cheeriest "Aye, aye, sir!" in the world. When there was nothing else to do, he kept up one song after another, as if to hide the discontent of the rest.

Of all the gloomy features of that gloomy afternoon, this obvious worry on the part of Long John appeared the worst.

We held a council in the cabin.

"Sir," said the captain, "if I risk another order, the whole ship'll come about our ears by the run. You see, sir, here it is. I get a rough answer, do I not? Well, if I speak back, pikes[5] will be going in two shakes. If I don't, Silver will see there's something under that and the game's up. Now we've only one man to rely on."

"And who is that?" asked the squire.

"Silver, sir," replied the captain. "He's as anxious as you and I to smother things up. This is a minor disagreement between him and his men. He'd soon talk

---

[5] Pikes are spears or other sharp-pointed weapons.

'em out of it if he had the chance. What I propose to do is to give him the chance. Let's allow the men an afternoon ashore. If they all go, why, we'll fight the ship. If they none of them go, well, then we hold the cabin and God defend the right. If some go, you mark my words, Silver'll bring 'em aboard again as mild as lambs."

It was so decided. Loaded pistols were served out to all the sure men. Hunter, Joyce, and Redruth were taken into our confidence. They received the news with less surprise and a better spirit than we had looked for. Then the captain went on deck and addressed the crew.

"My lads," said he, "we've had a hot day and are all tired and out of sorts. A turn ashore'll hurt nobody. The boats are still in the water. You can take the gigs, and as many as please can go ashore for the afternoon. I'll fire a gun half an hour before sundown."

I believe the silly fellows must have thought they would break their shins over treasure as soon as they were landed. For they all came out of their sulks in a moment and gave a cheer that started the echo in a far away hill. It sent the birds once more flying and screaming round the anchorage.

The captain was too bright to be in the way. He whipped out of sight in a moment, leaving Silver to arrange the party. I fancy it was as well he did so. Had he been on deck, he could no longer have pretended not to understand the situation. It was as plain as day.

Silver was the captain, and a mighty rebellious crew he had of it. The honest hands—and I was soon to see it proved that there were such on board—must have been very stupid fellows. Or rather, I suppose the truth was that all hands were affected by the example of the ringleaders. Some were more, some less. And a few, being good fellows in the main, could neither be led nor driven any further. It is one thing to be lazy and sneaky and quite another to take a ship and murder a number of innocent men.

At last, however, the party was made up. Six fellows

were to stay on board. The remaining thirteen, including Silver, began to **embark.**

Then it was that there came into my head the first of the mad ideas that contributed so much to save our lives. If six men were left by Silver, it was plain our party couldn't take and fight the ship. Since only six were left, it was equally plain that the cabin party had no present need of my help. It occurred to me at once to go ashore. In a jiffy I had slipped over the side and curled up in the bow of the nearest boat. Almost at the same moment, she shoved off.

No one took notice of me. Only the bow oar said, "Is that you, Jim? Keep your head down." But Silver looked sharply over from the other boat and called out to know if that was me. From that moment I began to regret what I had done.

The crews raced for the beach. The boat I was in had some start and was at once the lighter and the better manned. So she shot far ahead of her companion. The bow struck among the shoreside trees, and I caught a branch and swung myself out. I plunged into the nearest thicket while Silver and the rest were still a hundred yards behind. "Jim, Jim!" I heard Silver shouting.

But you may suppose I paid no attention. Jumping, ducking, and breaking through, I ran straight before my nose till I could run no longer.

Chapter 14

The First Blow

Vocabulary Preview

The following words appear in this chapter. Review the list and get to know the words before you read the chapter.

contorted—twisted; bent out of shape
craggy—rocky; rough
defy—dare; challenge
extricate—untangle; free
fiends—wicked people
missile—something fired or thrown at a target

I was so pleased at having given the slip to Long John that I began to enjoy myself. I looked around me with some interest in the strange land that I was in.

I had crossed a marshy stretch full of willows, bulrushes,[1] and strange, swampy trees. I had now come out upon the edge of an open piece of rolling, sandy country. It was about a mile long, dotted with a few pines. There were also a great number of **contorted** trees, not unlike the oak in growth but with pale leaves like willows. On the far side of the open stood one of the hills with two charming, **craggy** peaks shining brightly in the sun.

I now felt for the first time the joy of exploration. No one lived on the island. I had left behind my shipmates,

[1] Willows are trees or shrubs that usually have narrow leaves and slender, flexible branches. Bulrushes are tall, grasslike plants that grow in wet or marshy places.

and nothing lived in front of me but dumb animals and birds. I turned hither and thither among the trees.

Here and there were flowering plants, unknown to me. Here and there I saw snakes. One raised his head from a ledge of rock and hissed at me with a noise like the spinning of a top. Little did I suppose that he was a deadly enemy and that the noise was the famous rattle.

Then I came to a long thicket of these oak-like trees—live, or evergreen, oaks, I heard afterwards they should be called. They grew low along the sand like shrubs. The branches were curiously twisted, and the leaves grew close together like thatch.[2]

The thicket stretched down from the top of one of the sandy hills. As it went it spread and grew taller until it reached the margin of the broad reedy swamp. The nearest of the little rivers soaked its way through the marsh into the anchorage. The marsh was steaming in the strong sun. The outline of the Spy-glass trembled through the haze.

All at once a sort of bustle began among the bulrushes. A wild duck flew up with a quack and another followed. And soon over the whole surface of the marsh a great cloud of birds hung screaming and circling in the air.

I judged at once that some of my shipmates must be drawing near along the borders of the swamp. Nor was I mistaken. Soon I heard the very distant and low tones of a human voice. As I continued to give ear, the voice grew steadily louder and nearer.

This put me in a great fear, and I crawled under cover of the nearest live oak. I squatted there, listening, as silent as a mouse.

Another voice answered. Then the first voice—which I now recognized to be Silver's—once more took up the story. It ran on for a long while without stopping, only now and again interrupted by the other. By the sound, they must have been talking earnestly and almost fiercely. But no clear word came to my hearing.

---

[2] Thatch is plant material packed tightly as a covering for a roof.

At last the speakers seemed to have paused and perhaps to have sat down. Not only did they cease to draw any nearer. But the birds themselves began to grow more quiet and to settle again to their places in the swamp.

And now I began to feel that I was neglecting my business. I had been foolhardy to come ashore with these desperadoes. So the least I could do was to overhear them at their councils. My plain and obvious duty was to get as close as I could manage, under the favorable cover of the crouching trees.

I could tell the direction of the speakers pretty exactly and not only by the sound of their voices. I could see the behavior of the few birds that still hung in alarm above the heads of the intruders.

Crawling on all fours, I made steadily but slowly towards them. At last, I raised my head to an opening among the leaves. Then I could see clear down into a little green dell[3] beside the marsh. The clearing was closely set about with trees. There, Long John Silver and another of the crew stood face to face in conversation.

The sun beat full upon them. Silver had thrown his hat beside him on the ground. His great, smooth, blond face was all shining with heat. It was lifted to the other man's in a kind of appeal.

"Mate," Silver was saying, "it's because I thinks gold dust of you—gold dust, and you may lay to that! If I hadn't took to you like pitch,[4] do you think I'd have been here a-warning you? All's up—you can't make nor mend. It's to save your neck that I'm a-speaking. If one of the wild 'uns knew it, where would I be, Tom? Now, tell me, where would I be?"

"Silver," said the other man. I observed he was not only red in the face but spoke as hoarse as a crow. His voice shook, too, like a rope pulled tight.

"Silver," said he again, "you're old and you're honest,

---

[3] A dell is a little hollow or valley.
[4] Pitch is a dark, sticky substance such as tar.

or has the name for it. And you have money too, which
lots of poor sailors hasn't. And you're brave, or I'm
mistaken. And will you tell me you'll let yourself be led
away with that kind of a mess of swabs? Not you! As sure
as God sees me, I'd sooner lose my hand. If I turn against
my duty—"

And then all of a sudden he was interrupted by a
noise. I had found one of the honest hands. Well, here at
that same moment came news of another. Far away out in
the marsh there arose, all of a sudden, a sound like the
cry of anger. Then there was another on the back of it,
and then one horrid drawn-out scream. The rocks of the
Spy-glass re-echoed it twenty times.

The whole troop of marsh birds rose again with a loud
whirring sound, darkening heaven. Long after that death
yell was still ringing in my brain, silence had re-
established its empire. Only the rustle of the descending
birds and the boom of the distant surf disturbed the
drowsiness of the afternoon.

Tom had leaped at the sound, like a horse at the spur.
But Silver hadn't winked an eye. He stood where he was,
resting lightly on his crutch. He watched his companion
like a snake about to spring.

"John!" said the sailor, stretching out his hands.

"Hands off!" cried Silver, leaping back a yard, it
seemed to me. He had the speed and steadiness of a
trained gymnast.

"Hands off if you like, John Silver," said the other.
"It's a black conscience that can make you feared of me.
But, in heaven's name, tell me, what was that?"

"That?" replied Silver, smiling away but more
watchful than ever. His eye was a mere pinpoint in his big
face, but gleaming like a crumb of glass. "That? Oh, I
reckon that'll be Alan."

At this, poor Tom flashed out like a hero.

"Alan!" he cried. "Then rest his soul for a true
seaman! And as for you, John Silver, you've long been a
mate of mine. But you're a mate of mine no more. If I die

like a dog, I'll die in my duty. You've killed Alan, have you? Kill me, too, if you can. But I **defy** you."

And with that, this brave fellow turned his back directly on the cook and set off walking for the beach. But he wasn't destined to go far. With a cry, John seized the branch of a tree. He whipped the crutch out of his armpit and sent that crude **missile** hurtling through the air. It struck poor Tom point first. It hit with incredible violence right between the shoulders, in the middle of the back. Tom's hands flew up. He gave a sort of gasp and fell.

Whether he were injured much or little, none could ever tell. Likely enough—to judge from the sound—his back was broken on the spot. But he had no time given him to recover. Silver was agile as a monkey even without leg or crutch. He was on the sailor the next moment and had twice buried his knife up to the hilt in that defenseless body. From my place of hiding, I could hear him pant aloud as he struck the blows.

I don't know exactly what it is to faint. But I do know that for the next little while the whole world swam away from before me in a whirling mist. Silver and the birds and the tall Spy-glass hilltop went round and round and topsy-turvy before my eyes. All kinds of bells were ringing. Distant voices were shouting in my ear.

When I came again to myself, the monster had pulled himself together. His crutch was under his arm, his hat upon his head. Just before him Tom lay motionless upon the turf. But the murderer minded him not a whit. He cleansed his bloodstained knife upon a wisp of grass for a while.

Everything else was unchanged. The sun was still shining without mercy on the steaming marsh and the tall peak of the mountain. I could hardly persuade myself that murder had been actually done and a human life cruelly cut short a moment ago, before my eyes.

But now John put his hand into his pocket and brought out a whistle. He blew upon it several different blasts that rang far across the heated air. I couldn't tell the meaning of the signal, of course. But it instantly awoke my fears. More men would be coming. I might be discovered. They had already slain two of the honest people. After Tom and Alan, might not I come next?

Instantly I began to **extricate** myself and crawl back again to the more open part of the wood. I moved with what speed and silence I could manage. As I did so, I could hear hails coming and going between the old buccaneer and his comrades. This sound of danger lent me wings.

As soon as I was clear of the thicket, I ran as I never ran before. I hardly cared about the direction of my flight, so long as it led me away from the murderers. As I ran, fear grew and grew upon me until it turned into a kind of frenzy.

Indeed, could anyone be more entirely lost than I? When the gun fired, how should I dare to go down to the boats among those **fiends?** They were still smoking from their crime. Wouldn't the first of them who saw me wring my neck like a bird's? Wouldn't my absence itself be an evidence to them of my alarm, and therefore of my deadly knowledge?

It was all over, I thought. Goodbye to the *Hispaniola*. Goodbye to the squire, the doctor, the captain! There was nothing left for me but death by starvation or death by the hands of the mutineers.[5]

As I said, all this time I was still running. Without taking any notice, I had drawn near to the foot of the little hill with the two peaks. I had got into a part of the island where the live oaks grew more widely apart. Here they seemed more like forest trees in their height and size. Mixed with these were a few scattered pines, some fifty, some nearer seventy feet high. The air, too, smelled more fresh than down beside the marsh.

And here a fresh alarm brought me to a standstill with a thumping heart.

[5] Mutineers are those who try to mutiny, or overthrow, those in charge.

Chapter 15

The Man of the Island

Vocabulary Preview

The following words appear in this chapter. Review the list and get to know the words before you read the chapter.

adversary—opponent; challenger
apparition—ghostly figure; strange sight
hinder—hold back; block
pious—religious; devout
predicament—difficult or troublesome situation
solitude—aloneness; isolation

From the side of the hill, which was here steep and stony, a stream of gravel was knocked loose. It fell rattling and bounding through the trees. My eyes automatically turned in that direction. I saw a figure leap quickly behind the trunk of a pine.

What it was—whether bear or man or monkey—I could in no way tell. It seemed dark and shaggy; more I knew not. But the terror of this new **apparition** brought me to a standstill.

It seemed I was now cut off on both sides. Behind me were the murderers, before me this lurking mystery. And immediately I began to prefer the dangers that I knew to those I knew not. Silver himself appeared less terrible in contrast with this creature of the woods. I turned on my heel. Looking sharply behind me over my shoulder, I began to retrace my steps in the direction of the boats.

Instantly the figure reappeared. Making a wide circle, it began to head me off. I was tired, at any rate. But had I been as fresh as when I rose, I could see it was in vain for me to compete in speed with such an **adversary.**

From trunk to trunk the creature flitted like a deer. It ran manlike on two legs. But it was unlike any man that I had ever seen. It stooped almost double as it ran. Yet a man it was—I could no longer be in doubt about that.

I began to recall what I had heard of cannibals.[1] I was very near to calling for help. But the mere fact that he was a man, however wild, had somewhat reassured me. My fear of Silver began to grow in proportion.

Therefore, I stood still and cast about for some method of escape. As I was so thinking, the recollection of my pistol flashed into my mind. As soon as I remembered I wasn't defenseless, courage glowed again in my heart. I set my face firmly for this man of the island and walked briskly towards him.

He was hidden by this time behind another tree trunk. But he must have been watching me closely. As soon as I began to move in his direction, he reappeared and took a step to meet me. Then he hesitated, drew back, and came forward again. At last, to my wonder and confusion, he threw himself on his knees and held out his clasped hands.

At that I once more stopped.

"Who are you?" I asked.

"Ben Gunn," he answered. His voice sounded hoarse and awkward, like a rusty lock. "I'm poor Ben Gunn, I am. And I haven't spoke with a Christian these three years."

I could see now that he was a white man like myself and that his features were even pleasing. His skin was burnt by the sun wherever it was exposed. Even his lips were black. His fair eyes looked quite startling in so dark a face.

Of all the beggar-men that I had seen or imagined, he

---

[1] Cannibals are humans who eat the flesh of other humans.

was the chief for raggedness. He was clothed with tatters of old ship's canvas and old sea cloth. This extraordinary patchwork was all held together by a system of the most varied and unmatched fastenings—brass buttons, bits of stick, and loops of black gaskin.[2] About his waist he wore an old brass-buckled leather belt. That was the one solid thing in his whole costume.

"Three years!" I cried. "Were you shipwrecked?"

"Nay, mate," said he. "Marooned."

I had heard the word. I knew it stood for a horrible kind of punishment common enough among the buccaneers. The offender is put ashore on some deserted and distant island. He is given a little powder and some shot and then left behind.

"Marooned three years agone," he continued. "And lived on goats since then, and berries and oysters. Wherever a man is, says I, a man can do for himself. But, mate, my heart is sore for Christian diet. You wouldn't happen to have a piece of cheese about you, now? No? Well, many's the long night I've dreamed of cheese— toasted mostly—and woke up again and here I were."

"If ever I can get on board again," said I, "you shall have all the cheese you want."

All this time he had been feeling the stuff of my jacket. He smoothed my hands and looked at my boots. In the pauses of his speech he was generally showing a childish pleasure in the presence of a fellow creature. But at my last words he perked up into a kind of startled slyness.

"If ever you can get aboard again, says you?" he repeated. "Why, now, who's to **hinder** you?"

"Not you, I know," was my reply.

"And right you was," he cried. "Now you—what do you call yourself, mate?"

"Jim," I told him.

"Jim, Jim," says he, quite pleased apparently. "Well now, Jim, I've lived so rough you'd be ashamed to hear of

[2] A gaskin is a stocking.

it. Now, for instance, you wouldn't think I had had a **pious** mother—to look at me?" he asked.

"Why no, not in particular," I answered.

"Ah well," said he, "but I had—remarkably pious. And I was a well-mannered, pious boy. I could rattle off my catechism[3] so fast that you couldn't tell one word from another. And here's what it come to, Jim. And it begun with chuck-farthen[4] on the blessed gravestones!

"That's what it begun with, but it went further'n that. And so my mother told me and predicted the whole, she did, the pious woman! But it were Providence[5] that put me here. I've thought it all out on this here lonely island, and I'm back on religion.

"You won't catch me tasting rum so much. Just a thimbleful for luck, of course, the first chance I have. I'm bound I'll be good and I see the way to. And Jim,"—he looked all round him and lowered his voice to a whisper—"I'm rich."

I now felt sure that the poor fellow had gone crazy in his **solitude.** I suppose I must have shown the feeling in my face, for he repeated the statement hotly.

"Rich! Rich! I says. And I'll tell you what. I'll make a man of you, Jim. Ah, Jim, you'll bless your stars, you will, that you was the first that found me!"

And at this there came suddenly a lowering shadow over his face. He tightened his grasp upon my hand and raised a forefinger threateningly before my eyes.

"Now, Jim, you tell me true—that ain't Flint's ship?" he asked.

At this I had a happy thought. I began to believe I had found an ally and I answered him at once.

"It's not Flint's ship and Flint is dead. But I'll tell you true, as you ask me—there are some of Flint's hands aboard. Worse luck for the rest of us."

[3] A catechism is the basic principles of a religion in question and answer form.
[4] Chuck-farthen is a game in which players pitch coins to see who can get them closest to a marker. The winner gets to toss all the coins at a hole and keep those that go in.
[5] *Providence* means "God's plan" or "fate."

"Not a man—with one—leg?" he gasped.

"Silver?" I asked.

"Ah, Silver!" says he, "that were his name."

"He's the cook and the ringleader, too."

He was still holding me by the wrist and at that he gave it quite a wring.

"If you was sent by Long John," he said, "I'm as good as pork and I know it. But where was you, do you suppose?"

I had made up my mind in a moment. By way of answer I told him the whole story of our voyage and the **predicament** in which we found ourselves. He heard me with the sharpest interest. When I had done, he patted me on the head.

"You're a good lad, Jim," he said. "And you're all in a clove hitch,[6] ain't you? Well, you just put your trust in Ben Gunn. Ben Gunn's the man to do it. Would you think it likely, now, that your squire would prove a generous one in case of help—him being in a clove hitch, as you remark?"

I told him the squire was the most generous of men.

"Ay, but you see," replied Ben Gunn. "I didn't mean giving me a gate to keep and a suit of livery clothes[7] and such. That's not my mark, Jim. What I mean is, would he be likely to come down to the tune of, say, one thousand pounds out of money that's as good as a man's own already?"

"I'm sure he would," said I. "As it was, all hands were to share."

"*And* a passage home?" he added, with a look of great shrewdness.

"Why," I cried, "the squire's a gentleman. And besides, if we got rid of the others, we should want you to help work the vessel home."

"Ah," said he, "so you would." And he seemed very much relieved.

---

[6] *In a clove hitch* means "in a bind."
[7] A livery suit was a uniform worn by male servants.

"Now I'll tell you what," he went on. "So much I'll tell you and no more. I were in Flint's ship when he buried the treasure, he and six others—six strong seamen. They were ashore nearly a week and us standing off and on in the old *Walrus*.

"One fine day up went the signal. And here come Flint by himself in a little boat, his head done up in a blue scarf. The sun was getting up, and he looked deathly white about the cut-water. But there he was, you mind. And the six was all dead—dead and buried. How he done it, not a man aboard us could make out. It was battle, murder, and sudden death, leastways—him against six.

"Billy Bones was the mate. Long John, he was quartermaster. They asked Flint where the treasure was.

" 'Ah,' says Flint, 'you can go ashore if you like, and stay,' he says. 'But as for the ship, she'll sail—even against rough winds, by thunder!' That's what he said.

"Well I was in another ship three years back and we sighted this island. 'Boys,' said I, 'here's Flint's treasure. Let's land and find it.' The cap'n was displeased at that, but his mates were all of a mind and landed.

"Twelve days they looked for it, and every day they had the worse word for me. Until one fine morning, all hands went aboard. 'As for you, Benjamin Gunn,' they says, 'here's a musket,' they says, 'and a spade and a pick-axe. You can stay here and find Flint's money for yourself,' they says.

"Well, Jim, three years have I been here and not a bite of Christian diet from that day to this. But now, you look here. Look at me. Do I look like a man before the mast? No, says you. Nor I weren't neither, I says."

With that he winked and pinched me hard.

"Just you mention them words to your squire, Jim," he went on. "Nor he weren't, neither—that's the words. Three years he were the man of this island, light and dark, fair and rain. Sometimes he would, maybe, think upon a prayer (says you). And sometimes he would, maybe, think of his old mother, so be as she's alive (you'll say). But the most part of Gunn's time (this is what you'll say)—the most part of his time was took up with another matter. And then you'll give him a nip, like I do."

And he pinched me again, as though confiding in me. "Then," he continued, "then you'll up and you'll say this: Gunn is a good man (you'll say). And he puts a precious sight more confidence—a precious sight, mind that—in a gen'leman born than in these gen'lemen of fortune, having been one hisself."

"Well," I said, "I don't understand one word that you've been saying. But that's neither here nor there. For how am I to get on board?"

"Ah," said he, "that's the hitch for sure. Well, there's my boat, that I made with my two hands. I keep her under the white rock. If the worst comes to the worst, we might try that after dark. Hi!" he broke out, "what's that?"

For just then—although the sun had still an hour or two to run—all the echoes of the island awoke and bellowed to the thunder of a cannon.

"They've begun to fight!" I cried. "Follow me."

And I began to run towards the anchorage, my terrors all forgotten. Close at my side, the marooned man in his goatskins trotted easily and lightly.

"Left, left," says he. "Keep to your left hand, mate Jim! Under the trees with you! There's where I killed my first goat. They don't come down here now. They're all high up on them mountains for the fear of Benjamin Gunn.

"Ah! There's the cetemery." Cemetery, he must have meant. "You see the mounds? I come here and prayed nows and thens, when I thought maybe a Sunday would be about due. It weren't quite a chapel, but it seemed more solemn like. And then, says you, Ben Gunn was short-handed. No chaplain, nor so much as a Bible and flag, you says."

So he kept talking as I ran, neither expecting nor receiving any answer.

After a considerable pause, the cannon shot was followed by a volley[8] of small arms.

Another pause. Then, not a quarter of a mile in front of us, I beheld the Union Jack[9] flutter in the air above the woods.

[8] A volley is a discharge of several weapons, such as guns, at the same time.
[9] The Union Jack is the British flag.

PART IV: THE STOCKADE

Chapter 16 (Summary)

Narrative Continued by the Doctor:

How the Ship Was Abandoned

In the next three chapters Dr. Livesey, rather than Jim, narrates the story. Six mutineers were left on board when the others went ashore. The captain, the squire, and the doctor considered overpowering them and sailing the *Hispaniola* away. But there was no wind. To complicate matters, they discovered Jim Hawkins had slipped into a boat and gone ashore. They were afraid they would never see the boy alive again.

Waiting began to be a strain on the three gentlemen and their loyal companions. They decided that Hunter and the doctor should go ashore in the jolly boat to see what was going on.

After they landed, the doctor found the old stockade. He saw that it was near the top of a hill next to a spring of clear water. Dr. Livesey was glad to see the water since they hadn't had any on the ship. A log house with loopholes[1] for shooting in every side stood next to the spring. Around the house was a wide, cleared space. And around that was a six-foot fence with no doorway. It was an excellent fortress.

While looking at the stockade, Dr. Livesey heard the cry of a man being killed. He thought it must be Jim Hawkins. The doctor and Hunter immediately went back to the ship. They found the squire also upset by the cry. The doctor told the squire his plan.

Hunter brought the jolly boat under the stern of the schooner. The squire and the captain told the coxswain, Israel Hands, that they would shoot any mutineer who

---

[1] A loophole is a small hole or slit in a wall.

came above deck. Redruth stayed on guard to prevent the pirates from sneaking up through the forward hatch. For protection he had several loaded muskets and a mattress.

Joyce and the doctor loaded the small boat with powder, tins, muskets, bags of biscuits, kegs of pork, a cask of cognac, and the doctor's medicine chest. Once on the island, they carried those loads to the stockade. Joyce and Hunter—with half-a-dozen loaded muskets—stayed to guard fortress and supplies.

The doctor knew his group had one big advantage over Silver's group—guns. This is why he risked getting a second boatload of provisions. Upon arriving at the ship, he, the squire, and the captain filled the boat. They threw the guns and powder they couldn't carry into the water. Abraham Gray—one of the six mutineers on the ship— left his group and joined the captain. Then the squire, captain, doctor, Redruth, and Gray left the *Hispaniola* for the final trip to shore.

Chapter 17 (Summary)

Narrative Continued by the Doctor:

The Jolly Boat's Last Trip

On the last trip to the island, the jolly boat was heavily loaded with the five full-grown men—not to mention the supplies. And the tide was going out, making a strong rippling current. As a result, the boat was swept off course. As the men were struggling with the current and trying to keep from sinking, they saw a new danger.

Back at the *Hispaniola,* the mutineers were uncovering a long gun. Israel Hands was an experienced gunner and was preparing to fire at them. Since Squire Trelawney was the best shot in the jolly boat, the captain asked him to pick off the pirate. Trelawney fired his musket, but Hands stooped down and another sailor was hit instead.

The pirates who were on shore came swarming out of the woods. Those on the schooner fired at the jolly boat. That was the shot that Jim and Ben Gunn heard. But the ball passed over the heads of the men in the jolly boat.

At this time the small boat was very low in the water. The squire and Redruth tried to stop the boat in order to miss the cannon shot. In doing so, the jolly boat was swamped, and it sank in three feet of water. The people were all right, but three of the five guns and a lot of the supplies were under water. The men heard the pirates coming through the woods. They quickly waded to shore and left the sunken boat and supplies.

Chapter 18 (Summary)

Narrative Continued by the Doctor:

End of the First Day's Fighting

The group from the sunken jolly boat hurried toward the stockade. They could hear the voices of the buccaneers coming closer. Just as they reached the stockade, seven of the mutineers appeared. The squire and the doctor fired, and Hunter and Joyce also fired from within the stockade. One of the enemies fell and the rest turned and ran.

The men reached the stockade safely. Before they entered it, they went to check on the fallen enemy. While they rejoiced at their success, a pistol shot from the woods wounded old Redruth. The rest unleashed a volley of shots that scattered the mutineers again. Then they carried the seriously wounded gamekeeper back into the stockade and put him in the log house. The grieving squire sat by Redruth while the old man died.

The captain had brought the British flag from the ship, so they flew their colors over the log house. The doctor told the captain it would be months before another ship would set out to find them. The captain showed his worry about the supplies lasting that long. He regretted the loss of the supplies that went down in the jolly boat.

Again the pirates fired the cannon from the schooner. They seemed to be aiming at the flag, but the ball fell harmlessly into the stockade. The pirates fired the cannon again and again, but they did no real damage.

Later, when the tide had gone out, the captain felt that the supplies in the water were probably uncovered. Gray and Hunter went out to collect what they could. But the pirates had gotten there first and were carting everything away. And the pirates all had muskets, which they must have had hidden on the schooner.

The group in the stockade included Captain Smollett, Dr. Livesey, Squire Trelawney, seaman Gray, and the squire's servants, Hunter and Joyce. They figured that their supplies would last ten days if they ate very little each day.

Dr. Livesey wondered what had become of Jim Hawkins. Just then the men heard a call. Dr. Livesey looked out the door in time to see Jim climbing over the stockade wall to join them.

Chapter 19

Narrative Resumed by Jim Hawkins:

The Garrison in the Stockade

Vocabulary Preview

The following words appear in this chapter. Review the list and get to know the words before you read the chapter.

bombardment—forceful attack using missiles
demolishing—breaking into pieces; destroying
flourished—grew well; thrived
truce—temporary pause of warfare or unfriendliness by agreement; cease-fire

As soon as Ben Gunn saw the colors,[1] he came to a halt. He stopped me by the arm and sat down.

"Now," said he, "there's your friends, sure enough."

"Far more likely it's the mutineers," I answered.

"That!" he cried. "Why, in a place like this, where nobody puts in but gen'lemen of fortune, Silver would fly the Jolly Roger.[2] Don't make no doubt of that. No; that's your friends. There's been blows, too, and I reckon your friends has had the best of it. Here they are ashore in the old stockade that was made years and years ago by Flint. Ah, he was the man to have a head, was Flint! Except for rum, his match was never seen. He was afraid of none,

[1] *The colors* refers to the flag, in this case the British flag.
[2] The Jolly Roger is a pirate flag. It is black with a white skull and crossbones or other symbol of death.

not he. Only Silver—Silver was that genteel."[3]

"Well," said I, "that may be so, and so be it. All the more reason that I should hurry on and join my friends."

"Nay, mate," replied Ben, "not you. You're a good boy, or I'm mistaken. But you're only a boy, all told. Now, Ben Gunn is going to fly. Rum wouldn't bring me there, where you're going—not rum wouldn't. Not until I see your born gen'leman and gets it on his word of honor. And you won't forget my words! 'A precious sight (that's what you'll say), a precious sight more confidence'—and then nips him."

And he pinched me the third time with the same air of cleverness.

"And when Ben Gunn is wanted, you know where to find him, Jim. Just where you found him today. And him that comes is to have a white thing in his hand. And he's to come alone. Oh! And you'll say this: 'Ben Gunn,' says you, 'has reasons of his own.' "

"Well," said I, "I believe I understand. You have something to propose and you wish to see the squire or the doctor. You're to be found where I found you. Is that all?"

"And when? says you," Ben Gunn added. "Why, from about noon observation to about six bells."[4]

"Good," said I. "And now may I go?"

"You won't forget?" he inquired anxiously. "Precious sight, and reasons of his own, says you. Reasons of his own, that's the mainstay, as between man and man. Well, then"—still holding me—"I reckon you can go, Jim. And Jim, if you was to see Silver, you wouldn't go for selling Ben Gunn? Wild horses wouldn't draw it from you? No, says you. And if them pirates camp ashore, Jim, what would you say but there'd be widows in the morning?"

---

[3] *Genteel* usually means "noble" or "upper-class." Here *genteel* means "superior" or "best."

[4] At sea a bell is rung at every half-hour to mark the time of a watch or guard duty. Six bells is the sixth half-hour of the watch. So six bells would be three hours. This means Ben Gunn would be at the spot from about noon till about 3 p.m.

Here he was interrupted by a loud report. A cannonball came tearing through the trees. It pitched into the sand not a hundred yards from where we two were talking. The next moment each of us had taken to his heels in a different direction.

For a good hour to come, frequent reports shook the island. Balls kept crashing through the woods. I moved from hiding place to hiding place, always pursued by those terrifying missiles. Or so it seemed to me.

But toward the end of the **bombardment,** I had begun to pluck up my courage again in a way. I still didn't dare venture in the direction of the stockade, where the balls fell most often. However, after a long detour to the east, I crept down along the shoreside trees.

The sun had just set. The sea breeze was rustling and tumbling in the woods and ruffling the gray surface of the anchorage. The tide was far out and great sections of sand lay uncovered. After the heat of the day, the air chilled me through my jacket.

The *Hispaniola* still lay where she had anchored. But sure enough there was the Jolly Roger—the black flag of piracy—flying from her peak. Even as I looked, there came another red flash and another report that sent the echoes clattering. One more round-shot whistled through the air. It was the last of the cannonade.

I lay for some time, watching the bustle that followed the attack. Men were **demolishing** something with axes on the beach near the stockade—the poor jolly boat, I discovered afterwards. Away near the mouth of the river, a great fire was glowing among the trees. Between that point and the ship, one of the gigs kept coming and going. The men, whom I had seen so gloomy, shouted at the oars like children. But there was a sound in their voices that suggested they'd been drinking rum.

Finally, I thought I might return toward the stockade. I was pretty far down on the low, sandy spit.[5] That spit encloses the anchorage on one side and is joined to

---

[5] A spit is a narrow point of land that extends into a body of water.

Skeleton Island when the tide is low.

Now, as I rose to my feet, I saw a single rock, pretty high and unusually white in color. It was some distance farther down the spit and rising from among low bushes. It occurred to me that this might be the white rock of which Ben Gunn had spoken. Some day or other a boat might be wanted, and I would know where to look for one.

Then I skirted through the woods until I had regained the rear, or shoreward side, of the stockade. I was soon warmly welcomed by the faithful party.

I had soon told my story and begun to look about me. The log house was made of unsquared trunks of pine—roof, walls, and floor. The latter stood in several places as much as a foot or a foot and a half above the surface of the sand.

There was a porch at the door. Under this porch, the little spring welled up into an artificial basin of a rather odd kind. It was no other than a great ship's kettle of iron with the bottom knocked out. The kettle was sunk in the sand "to her bearings," as the captain said.

Little had been left besides the framework of the house. But in one corner there was a stone slab laid down for use as hearth. There was an old rusty iron basket to contain the fire.

The slopes of the hill and all the inside of the stockade had been cleared of timber to build the house. We could see by the stumps what a fine and lofty grove had been destroyed. Most of the soil had been washed away or buried in drift after the removal of the trees.

Only where the streamlet ran down from the kettle a thick bed of moss and some ferns and little creeping bushes were still green in the sand. Very close around the stockade—too close for defense, they said—the woods still **flourished** high and dense. It was all fir on the land side, but towards the sea there was a large mix of live oaks.

The cold evening breeze of which I have spoken

whistled through every gap of the rough buildings. The breeze sprinkled the floor with a constant rain of sand. There was sand in our eyes, sand in our teeth, and sand in our suppers. Sand even danced in the spring at the bottom of the kettle. It looked for all the world like porridge beginning to boil.

Our chimney was a square hole in the roof. Only a little part of the smoke found its way out. The rest swirled around the house and kept us coughing and wiping our eyes.

Add to this that the new man, Gray, had his face tied up in a bandage. He'd been cut while breaking away from the mutineers back on the ship. And poor old Tom Redruth was still unburied. He lay along the wall, stiff and stark under the Union Jack.

If we had been allowed to sit doing nothing, we should all have fallen into the blues. But Captain Smollett was never the man for that. He called all hands up before him and divided us up into watches. The doctor, Gray, and I, for one; the squire, Hunter, and Joyce for the other.

Tired as we all were, two were sent out for firewood. Two more were set to dig a grave for Redruth. The doctor was named cook. I was put guard at the door. The captain himself went from one to another. He kept up our spirits, lending a hand wherever it was wanted.

From time to time, the doctor came to the door for a little air and to rest his eyes, which were almost smoked out of his head. Whenever he did so, he had a word for me.

"That man Smollett," he said once, "is a better man than I am. And when I say that, it means a great deal, Jim."

Another time he came and was silent for a while. Then he put his head on one side and looked at me.

"Is this Ben Gunn a man?" he asked.

"I don't know, sir," said I. "I'm not very sure whether he's sane."

"If there's any doubt about the matter, he is," replied

the doctor. "Jim, the man has been three years biting his nails on a desert island. He can't expect to appear as sane as you or me. It's not human nature. Was it cheese you said he had a fancy for?"

"Yes, sir, cheese," I answered.

"Well, Jim," says he. "Just see the good that comes of being dainty in your food. You've seen my snuffbox, haven't you? And you never saw me take snuff.[6] The reason is that in my snuffbox I carry a piece of Parmesan cheese.[7] It's a cheese made in Italy and very nutritious. Well, that's for Ben Gunn!"

Before supper was eaten, we buried old Tom in the sand. We stood around him for a while bareheaded in the breeze. A good deal of firewood had been got in, but not enough for the captain's fancy. He shook his head over it and told us we "must get back to this tomorrow rather livelier."

We ate our pork and each of us had a good stiff glass of brandy grog. Then the three chiefs got together in a corner to discuss our chances.

It appeared they were at their wits' end what to do. The stores were so low that we would have been starved into surrender long before help came. But it was decided our best hope was to kill off the buccaneers until they either hauled down their flag or ran away with the *Hispaniola*.

From nineteen they were already reduced to fifteen. Two others were wounded. One, at least—the man shot beside the gun—was severely wounded if he were not dead. Every time we had a crack at them, we were to take it with the utmost care, saving our own lives. And besides that, we had two able allies—rum and the climate.

As for the first, we could hear them roaring and singing late into the night. And this though we were about half a mile away. As for the second, the doctor bet his wig that half of them would be on their backs before a

---

[6] Snuff is a finely ground tobacco used for snorting up the nose.
[7] Parmesan cheese is a hard, dry, flavorful cheese.

week. The mutineers were camped in the marsh and not provided with medications.

"So," the doctor added, "if we're not all shot down first, they'll be glad to be packing in the schooner. It's still a ship and they can get to buccaneering again, I suppose."

"First ship that ever I lost," said Captain Smollett.

I was dead tired, as you may fancy. When I got to sleep—which was not till after a great deal of tossing—I slept like a log of wood.

The rest had long been up when I was awakened by a bustle and the sound of voices. They had already had breakfast and increased the pile of firewood by about half as much again.

"Flag of **truce!**" I heard someone say. Then immediately after, with a cry of surprise, "Silver himself!"

And at that, up I jumped. Rubbing my eyes, I ran to a loophole in the wall.

Chapter 20 (Summary)

Silver's Embassy[1]

There were two men outside the stockade. One of them was waving a white cloth and the other was Long John Silver. Captain Smollett suspected a trick. He set men at guard on all sides of the log building. Then he asked Silver what he wanted.

Long John Silver said the men had chosen him captain after Smollett had "deserted" the ship. He said he wanted to reach some kind of agreement. Smollett said they had nothing to discuss. But Silver threw his crutch over the stockade fence and managed to climb over.

Silver struggled to climb up the steep hillside to the log house. His crutch was helpless in the soft sand. At last he arrived at the building. He complimented the captain on having made a successful attack during the night. Silver warned that it would never happen again because the mutineers would now stand watch.

The captain didn't know what Silver was talking about. But Jim figured that Ben Gunn must have paid the pirates a visit during the night. Now there was one less buccaneer to deal with—fourteen in all.

Long John Silver wanted the treasure map. He said that he had never meant anyone any harm. He wanted the party in the stockade to give up the map and stop shooting at the buccaneers. Then, he said, they could come back on the schooner. Silver said that he would put them ashore wherever they wanted to go. Or they would divide up the supplies and send another ship to pick them up.

The captain made a different offer. He said that Silver and his men could give up. Then he would put them all in irons[2] and take them back to a fair trial. The pirates

---

[1] An embassy is made up of official messengers who represent a certain group.

[2] Prisoners were often put in leg irons to prevent their escape.

couldn't find the treasure, Smollett said, and they didn't know how to sail the ship. Silver and the captain threatened to kill each other the next time they met.

Because of the soft sand, Silver couldn't get up from where he sat. No one would help him. Silver had to crawl along the sand to the porch, where he could pull himself up and use his crutch again. Then the pirate spat in the spring and left in a fury.

Chapter 21

The Attack

Vocabulary Preview

The following words appear in this chapter. Review the list and get to know the words before you read the chapter.

anxiety—nervousness; worry
assailant—attacker
clambering—climbing with difficulty; scrambling
interval—period of time; break

As soon as Silver disappeared, the captain—who had been closely watching him—turned towards the interior of the house. He found not a man of us at his post but Gray. It was the first time we had ever seen him angry.

"Quarters!" he roared. And then as we all slunk back to our places, he said, "Gray, I'll put your name in the log.[1] You've stood by your duty like a seaman. Mr. Trelawney, I'm surprised at you, sir. Doctor, I thought you had worn the king's coat! If that was how you served at Fontenoy,[2] sir, you'd have been better in your bunk."

The doctor's watch were all back at their loopholes. The rest were busy loading the spare muskets. You may be certain every one had a red face and a flea in his ear,[3] as the saying is.

---

[1] A log is a record of speeds and events of a ship's voyage.
[2] Fontenoy was the site of a French battle in 1745. English troops fought with the French.
[3] *A flea in one's ear* means "an irritating warning or hint of something."

The captain looked on for a while in silence. Then he spoke.

"My lads," said he, "I've given Silver an earful. I pitched it in red-hot on purpose. Before the hour's out we shall be boarded, as he said. We're outnumbered, I needn't tell you that. But we fight in shelter. And a minute ago I should have said we fought with discipline. I've no doubt at all that we can whip them, if you choose."

Then he went the rounds and saw, as he said, that all was clear.

On the two short sides of the house—east and west—there were only two loopholes. On the south side where the porch was, two again. And on the north side, five. There were twenty muskets for the seven of us. The firewood had been built into four piles—tables, you might say—one about the middle of each side. On each of these tables some ammunition and four loaded muskets were laid ready to the hand of the defenders. In the middle, the cutlasses were lined up.

"Toss out the fire," said the captain. "The chill is past and we mustn't have smoke in our eyes."

The iron fire-basket was carried bodily out by Mr. Trelawney. The embers were smothered among sand.

"Hawkins hasn't had his breakfast. Hawkins, help yourself, and back to your post to eat it," continued Captain Smollett. "Lively now, my lad. You'll want it before you've done. Hunter, serve out a round of brandy to all hands."

And while this was going on, the captain completed in his own mind the plan of defense.

"Doctor, you will take the door," he continued. "See, and don't expose yourself. Keep within and fire through the porch. Hunter, take the east side, there. Joyce, you stand by the west, my man. Mr. Trelawney, you're the best shot. You and Gray will take this long north side, with the five loopholes. It's there the danger is. If they can get up to it and fire in upon us through our own ports, things would begin to look dirty. Hawkins, neither you nor I are much account at the shooting. We'll stand by to load and give a hand."

As the captain had said, the chill was past. Soon the sun had climbed above our circle of trees. It fell with all its force above the clearing and drank up the mist at a gulp. Soon the sand was baking and the resin melting in the logs of the blockhouse.[4] Jackets and coats were flung aside. Shirts were thrown open at the neck and rolled up to the shoulders. We stood there, each at his post, in a fever of heat and **anxiety.**

An hour passed away.

"Hang them!" said the captain. "This is as dull as the doldrums.[5] Gray, whistle for a wind."

And just at that moment came the first news of the attack.

"If you please, sir," said Joyce, "if I see anyone, am I to fire?"

"I told you so!" cried the captain.

"Thank you, sir," replied Joyce, with the same quiet civility.

Nothing followed for a time, but the remark had set us all on the alert. We strained our eyes and ears. The musketeers had their pieces balanced in their hands. The captain was out in the middle of the blockhouse, with his mouth very tight and a frown on his face.

So some seconds passed, till suddenly Joyce whipped up his musket and fired. The report had barely died away before it was repeated and repeated from without in a scattering volley. Like a string of geese, shot rang behind shot from every side of the blockhouse.

Several bullets struck the log house, but not one entered. As the smoke cleared away and vanished, the stockade and the woods around it looked as quiet and empty as before. Not a branch waved. Not the gleam of a

---

[4] Resin is pine sap. A blockhouse is a structure for military defense. In this case, it is the log building.

[5] The doldrums are ocean regions near the equator. There are usually calms, meaning the complete lack of wind, in the doldrums.

musket barrel gave away the presence of our foes.

"Did you hit your man?" asked the captain.

"No, sir," replied Joyce. "I believe not, sir."

"Next best thing to tell the truth," muttered Captain Smollett. "Load his gun, Hawkins. How many would you say there were on your side, doctor?"

"I know exactly," said Dr. Livesey. "Three shots were fired on this side. I saw the three flashes—two close together, one farther to the west."

"Three!" repeated the captain. "And how many on yours, Mr. Trelawney?"

But this was not so easily answered. There had come many from the north—seven by the squire's count; eight or nine according to Gray. From the east and west only a single shot had been fired. Therefore, it was plain that the attack would be developed from the north. On the other three sides, we were only to be distracted by a few shots.

But Captain Smollett made no change in his arrangements. If the mutineers succeeded in crossing the stockade, he argued, they would take possession of any unprotected loophole. They would shoot us down like rats in our own stronghold.

We didn't have much time for thought. Suddenly, with a loud "Huzza!" a little cloud of pirates leaped from the woods on the north side. They ran straight at the stockade. At the same moment, the fire was once more opened from the woods. A rifle ball sang through the doorway and knocked the doctor's musket into bits.

The boarders swarmed over the fence like monkeys. Squire and Gray fired again and yet again. Three men fell, one forward into the enclosure, two back on the outside. But of these, one was evidently more frightened than hurt. He was on his feet again in a moment and instantly disappeared among the trees.

Two men had bit the dust. One had fled. Four had made good their footing inside our defenses. From the shelter of the woods, seven or eight men—each evidently supplied with several muskets—kept up a hot though useless fire on the log house.

The four who had boarded made straight before them for the building, shouting as they ran. The men among the trees shouted back to encourage them. Several shots were fired. But in the hurry of the marksmen, not one shot appeared to have any effect. In a moment, the four pirates had swarmed up the mound and were upon us.

The head of Job Anderson, the boatswain, appeared at the middle loophole.

"At 'em, all hands—all hands!" he roared in a voice of thunder.

At that same moment, another pirate grasped Hunter's musket by the muzzle. He wrenched the musket from Hunter's hands and plucked it through the loophole. With one stunning blow, the pirate laid the poor fellow senseless on the floor. Meanwhile, a third ran unharmed all round the house. He appeared suddenly in the doorway and fell with his cutlass on the doctor.

Our position was suddenly turned around. A moment ago we were firing under cover at an exposed enemy. Now it was we who lay uncovered and couldn't return a blow.

The log house was full of smoke, to which we owed our temporary safety. Cries and confusion, the flashes and reports of pistol shots, and one loud groan rang in my ears.

"Out, lads, out, and fight 'em in the open! Cutlasses!" cried the captain.

I snatched a cutlass from the pile. Someone snatched another at the same time. I received a cut across the knuckles which I hardly felt. I dashed out the door into the clear sunlight. Someone was close behind, I knew not whom. Right in front, the doctor was pursuing his **assailant** down the hill. Just as my eyes fell upon him, the doctor beat down the man's guard. He sent the pirate sprawling on his back, with a great slash across the face.

"Round the house, lads! Round the house!" cried the captain. Even in the hurly-burly, I noticed a change in his voice.

Mechanically I obeyed. I turned eastward and ran round the corner of the house with my cutlass raised. Next moment, I was face to face with Anderson. He roared aloud and his sword went up above his head, flashing in the sunlight. I had no time to be afraid. As the blow still hung in the air, I leaped to one side. I missed my footing in the soft sand and rolled headlong down the slope.

When I had first charged out the door, the other mutineers had been already swarming up the palisade[6] to make an end of us. One man in a red nightcap and with his cutlass in his mouth had even got to the top and thrown a leg across.

Well, the **interval** had been so short that when I found my feet again, all was in the same position. The fellow in the red nightcap was still halfway over. Another was still just showing his head above the top of the stockade. And yet—in this breath of time—the fight was over and the victory was ours.

Gray had been following close behind me. He had cut down the big boatswain before the scoundrel had time to recover from his lost blow. Another had been shot at a loophole in the very act of firing into the house. He now lay in agony, the pistol still smoking in his hand. A third the doctor had disposed of at a blow, as I had seen. Of the four who had scaled the palisade, only one wasn't accounted for. He had left his cutlass on the field and was now **clambering** out again with the fear of death upon him.

"Fire—fire from the house!" cried the doctor. "And you, lads, back into cover."

But his words were ignored. No shot was fired and the last boarder made good his escape. He disappeared with the rest into the woods. In three seconds nothing remained of the attacking party but the five who had fallen. Four were on the inside and one on the outside of the palisade.

---

[6] A palisade is a fence.

The doctor and Gray and I ran full speed for shelter. The survivors would soon be back where they had left their muskets. At any moment the firing might begin again.

The house was by this time somewhat cleared of smoke. We saw at a glance the price we had paid for victory. Hunter lay beside his loophole, stunned. Joyce was by him, shot through the head, never to move again. Right in the center, the squire was supporting the captain, one as pale as the other.

"The captain's wounded," said Mr. Trelawney.

"Have they run?" asked Mr. Smollett.

"All that could, you may be sure," replied the doctor. "But there's five of them will never run again."

"Five!" cried the captain. "Come, that's better. Five against three leaves us four to nine. That's better odds than we had at starting. We were seven to nineteen then. Or we thought we were, and that's as bad to bear."[7]

---

[7] The mutineers were soon only eight in number. The man shot by Mr. Trelawney on board the schooner died that same evening of his wound. But of course this wasn't known till after by the faithful party.

PART V: MY SEA ADVENTURE

Chapter 22

How I Began My Sea Adventure

Vocabulary Preview

The following words appear in this chapter. Review the list and get to know the words before you read the chapter.

dwindled—faded away; slowly disappeared
lingered—held on; stayed on
portable—movable; able to be carried
precautions—safeguards; measures taken to prevent harm
propulsion—push; driving force
scheme—plan; idea

There was no return of the mutineers—not so much as another shot out of the woods. They had "got their rations for that day," as the captain put it. We had the place to ourselves and a quiet time to look to the wounded and get dinner.

Squire and I cooked outside in spite of the danger. Even outside, we could hardly tell what we were at. The loud groans that reached us from the doctor's patients were horrible.

Out of the eight men who had fallen in the action, only three still breathed—the pirate who had been shot at the loophole, Hunter, and Captain Smollett. Of these, the first two were as good as dead. Indeed, the mutineer died under the doctor's knife.

Do what we could, Hunter never recovered

consciousness in this world. He **lingered** all day, breathing loudly. He sounded like the old buccaneer at home in his apoplectic fit. But the bones of his chest had been crushed by the blow and his skull fractured in falling. Some time in the following night—without sign or sound—he went to his Maker.

As for the captain, his wounds were serious indeed, but not dangerous. No organ was fatally injured. Anderson's ball—for it was Job Anderson that shot him first—had broken his shoulder blade and touched the lung, not badly. The second ball had only torn and displaced some muscles in the calf. He was sure to recover, the doctor said. But in the meantime, and for weeks to come, he must not walk or move his arm. Nor must he so much as speak when he could help it.

My own accidental cut across the knuckles was a flea bite. Dr. Livesey patched it up with plaster and pulled my ears for me into the bargain.

After dinner, the squire and the doctor sat by the captain's side a while in conference. When they had talked to their hearts' content, it was a little past noon. The doctor took up his hat and pistols, strapped on a cutlass, and put the chart in his pocket. With a musket on his shoulder, he crossed the palisade on the north side. Then he set off briskly through the trees.

Gray and I were sitting together at the far end of the blockhouse, to be out of earshot of our officers' meeting. Gray took his pipe out of his mouth and fairly forgot to put it back again. He was that thunderstruck at this sight.

"Why, in the name of Davy Jones,"[1] said he. "Is Dr. Livesey mad?"

"Why no," said I. "He's about the last of this crew for that, I take it."

"Well, shipmate," said Gray, "mad he may not be. But if *he's* not, you mark my words, *I* am."

"I take it the doctor has his idea," replied I. "If I'm

---

[1] Davy Jones is the legendary spirit of the sea. The bottom of the ocean, where sunken ships and drowned sailors ended up, is called Davy Jones' Locker.

right, he's going now to see Ben Gunn."

I was right, as appeared later. But in the meantime, the house was stifling hot. And the little patch of sand inside the palisade was ablaze with midday sun. I began to get another thought into my head, which was not by any means so right.

What I began to do was to envy the doctor, walking in the cool shadow of the woods. He had the birds about him and the pleasant smell of the pines. All the while I sat grilling, with my clothes stuck to the hot resin. There was so much blood around me and so many poor dead bodies lying all around that I took a disgust of the place. The feeling was almost as strong as fear.

I washed out the blockhouse and then washed up the things from dinner. The whole time this disgust and envy kept growing stronger and stronger. At last, I was near the bread bag and no one was observing me. I took the first step towards my escape and filled both pockets of my coat with biscuits.

I was a fool, if you like. Certainly I was going to do a foolish, over-bold act. But I was determined to do it with all the **precautions** in my power. Should anything happen to me, these biscuits would at least keep me from starving till far on in the next day.

The next thing I laid hold of was a pair of pistols. I already had a powder horn[2] and bullets. So I felt myself well supplied with arms.

As for the **scheme** I had in my head, it wasn't a bad one in itself. I was to go down the sandy spit that divides the anchorage on the east from the open sea. I would find the white rock I had noticed last evening. Then I would find out whether it was there or not that Ben Gunn had hidden his boat.

It was a thing quite worth doing, as I still believe. But I was certain I wouldn't be allowed to leave the enclosure. So my only plan was to take French leave[3] and slip out

---

[2] A powder horn is a flask for carrying gunpowder. It is sometimes made from a cow horn.

[3] French leave is leaving without permission.

when nobody was watching. And that was so bad a way of doing it that it made the thing itself wrong. But I was only a boy and I had made my mind up.

Well, as things at last fell out, I found an excellent opportunity. The squire and Gray were busy helping the captain with his bandages. The coast was clear. I made a bolt for it over the stockade and into the thicket of trees. Before my absence was noticed, I was out of sound of my companions.

This was my second mistake, and far worse than the first. For I left only two able-bodied men to guard the house. But like the first mistake, it was a help towards saving all of us.

I took my way straight for the east coast of the island. I was determined to go down the sea side of the spit to avoid all chance of being seen from the anchorage. It was already late in the afternoon, although still warm and sunny.

As I continued to thread through the tall woods, I could hear from far before me the nonstop thunder of the surf. I could also hear a certain tossing of leaves and grinding of branches. This showed me the sea breeze had set in stronger than usual. Soon, cool currents of air began to reach me. A few steps farther, I came forth into the open borders of the grove. I saw the sea lying blue and sunny to the horizon and the surf tumbling and tossing its foam along the beach.

I've never seen the sea quiet around Treasure Island. The sun might blaze overhead, the air be without a breath, the surface smooth and blue. But still these great rollers would be running along all the outer coast, thundering and thundering by day and night. I hardly believe there is one spot on the island where a man would be out of earshot of their noise.

I walked along beside the surf with great enjoyment. When I thought I had gotten far enough to the south, I took the cover of some thick bushes. I crept carefully up to the ridge of the spit.

Behind me was the sea, in front the anchorage. The sea breeze was already at an end. It was as though the breeze had blown itself out sooner by its unusual violence. It had been followed by light, changing winds from the south and southeast. These winds were carrying great banks of fog.

The anchorage—under lee of Skeleton Island—lay still and heavy as when first we entered it. In the unbroken mirror, the *Hispaniola* was pictured exactly from the top of the mast to the water line. The Jolly Roger was shown hanging from her peak.

Alongside lay one of the gigs. Silver was in the stern—him I could always recognize. A couple of men were leaning over the stern bulwarks, one of them with a red cap. He was the very rogue I had seen some hours before climbing over the palisade. Apparently they were talking and laughing. Of course, at that distance— upwards of a mile—I could hear no word of what was said.

All at once there began the most horrid, unearthly screaming. At first I was startled badly. However, I soon remembered the voice of Silver's bird, Captain Flint. I even thought I could make out the bird by her bright feathers as she sat perched upon her master's wrist.

Soon after, the jolly boat shoved off and pulled for shore. Then the man with the red cap and his comrade went below by the cabin staircase.

Just about the same time, the sun had gone down behind the Spy-glass. As the fog was collecting rapidly, it began to grow dark in earnest. I saw I must lose no time if I were to find Ben Gunn's boat that evening.

The white rock—visible enough above the brush— was still some eighth of a mile further down the spit. It took me a good while to get to it, for I had to crawl through the brush, often on all fours. Night had almost come when I laid my hand on the rock's rough sides.

Right below the white rock there was an extremely small hollow of green grass. The hollow was hidden by banks and a thick underbrush about knee-deep that grew there very plentifully. Sure enough, in the center of the dell was a little tent of goatskins. It looked like the tents the gypsies carry about with them in England.

I dropped into the hollow and lifted the side of the tent. There was Ben Gunn's boat—homemade if ever anything was homemade. It had a rude, lopsided framework of tough wood. Stretched upon that was a covering of goatskin, with the hair inside.

The boat was extremely small, even for me. I can hardly imagine that it could have floated with a full-sized man. There was one thwart set as low as possible and a kind of stretcher in the bows. There was a double paddle for **propulsion.**

I hadn't then seen a coracle[4] such as the ancient Britons made. But I have seen one since. I can give you no better idea of Ben Gunn's boat than by saying it was like the first and the worst coracle ever made by man. But it certainly possessed the great advantage of the coracle— it was very light and **portable.**

Well, now that I had found the boat, you would have thought that for once I had had enough of acting irresponsibly. But in the meantime, I had another idea. And I had become so stubbornly fond of the idea that I believe I would have carried it out in front of Captain Smollett himself.

My plan was to slip out under cover of the night, cut the *Hispaniola* adrift, and let her go ashore where she pleased. I had quite made up my mind that the mutineers wanted nothing more than to up anchor and away to sea. Especially after being beat off that morning. This, I thought, would be a fine thing to prevent. I had seen how they left their watchmen without a boat. So I thought my plan might be done with little risk.

Down I sat to wait for darkness. I made a hearty meal of biscuit. It was a night out of ten thousand for my

---

[4] A coracle is a boat made of waterproof material stretched over a lightweight wooden frame.

purpose. The fog had now buried all heaven. As the last rays of daylight **dwindled** and disappeared, absolute blackness settled down on Treasure Island. At last, I shouldered the coracle and groped and stumbled my way out of the hollow. By then there were but two points visible on the whole anchorage.

One was the great fire on shore, which the defeated, drunk pirates lay by in the swamp. The other—a mere blur of light upon the darkness—indicated the position of the anchored ship. She had swung round to the ebb, and her bow was now towards me. The only lights on board were in the cabin. What I saw was merely a reflection on the fog of the strong rays that flowed from the stern window.

The tide had been going out for some time, and I had to wade through a long belt of swampy sand. I sank several times above the ankle before I came to the edge of the retreating water. I waded a little way in. With some strength and skill I set my coracle on the surface, keel downwards.

Chapter 23

The Ebb-tide Runs

The coracle was a very safe boat for a person of my height and weight. I had plenty of reason to know this before I was done with her. She was both **buoyant** and clever in a seaway. But she was the most lopsided craft to manage. Do as you please, she always made more leeway[1] than anything else. Turning round and round was the maneuver she was best at. Even Ben Gunn himself has admitted that she was "curious to handle till you knew her way."

Certainly I didn't know her way. She turned in every direction but the one I tried to go. The most part of the time we were going sideways. I'm very sure I never should have made it to the ship at all except for the tide.

---

[1] *Made leeway* means the coracle drifted to the side away from the wind and from the desired course.

By good fortune—paddle as I pleased—the tide was still sweeping me along. And there lay the *Hispaniola* right in the way, hardly to be missed.

First she **loomed** before me like a blot of something blacker than darkness. Then her spars and hull began to take shape. The next moment, as it seemed—for the farther I went the brisker grew the current of the ebb—I was alongside of her hawser and had laid hold.

The anchor rope was as **taut** as a bowstring—so strong she pulled upon her anchor. All round the hill, in the blackness, the rippling current bubbled and chattered like a little mountain stream. One cut with my sea knife and the *Hispaniola* would go humming down the tide.

So far so good. But then I remembered that a taut anchor rope suddenly cut is a thing as dangerous as a kicking horse. I knew what would happen if I were so foolhardy as to cut the *Hispaniola* from her anchor. Ten to one, I and the coracle would be knocked clean out of the water.

This brought me to a full stop. If fortune hadn't again particularly favored me, I should have had to abandon my plan. But light winds that had begun blowing from the southeast and south had hauled around after nightfall into the southwest.

Just while I was thinking this over, a puff came and caught the *Hispaniola* and forced her up into the current. To my great joy, I felt the rope **slacken** in my grasp. The hand by which I held it dipped for a second under water.

With that, I made my mind up. I took out my knife, opened it with my teeth, and cut one strand after another till the vessel only swung by two strands. Then I lay quiet, waiting to **sever** these last when the strain should be once more lightened by a breath of wind.

All this time I had heard the sound of loud voices from the cabin. But to say the truth, my mind had been entirely taken up with other thoughts. So I had scarcely given ear. Now, however, I had nothing else to do. I began to pay more attention.

One voice I recognized was the coxswain, Israel Hands. He was the one who had been Flint's gunner in former days. The other was my friend of the red nightcap, of course. Both men were plainly the worse for drink, and they were still drinking. Even while I was listening, one of them gave a drunken cry. He opened the stern window and threw something out which I guessed to be an empty bottle.

But they weren't only tipsy. It was plain they were furiously angry. Oaths flew like hailstones. Every now and then there came forth such an explosion as I thought was sure to end in blows. But each time the quarrel passed off. The voices grumbled lower for a while until the next crisis came. Then that one in its turn passed away without result.

On shore, I could see the glow of the great campfire burning warmly through the shoreside trees. Someone was singing a dull, old, droning sailor's song with a droop and a quaver at the end of every verse. It seemed there was no end to it at all. I had heard it on the voyage more than once and remembered these words:

"But one man of her crew alive,
Which put to sea with seventy-five."

I thought the tune was rather too sadly appropriate for a company that had met such cruel losses in the morning. But from what I saw, all these buccaneers were indeed as **callous** as the sea they sailed on.

At last the breeze came. The schooner moved sideways and drew nearer in the dark. I felt the anchor rope slacken once more. With a good, tough effort I cut the last fibers through.

The breeze had but little effect on the coracle. I was almost instantly swept against the bow of the *Hispaniola*. At the same time, the *Hispaniola* began to turn upon her heel. Spinning slowly, she turned end for end across the current.

I struggled like a fiend, for I expected every moment

to sink. I found I couldn't push the coracle directly off. So I now shoved straight behind the ship. Finally, I was clear of my dangerous neighbor. Just as I gave the last push, my hands came across a light cord that was trailing overboard across the side. Instantly I grasped it.

Why I should have done so I can hardly say. It was at first mere instinct. But once I had it in my hands and found it attached to the ship, curiosity began to get the upper hand. I decided I should have one look through the cabin window.

I pulled in hand over hand on the cord. When I judged myself near enough, I rose at enormous risk to about half my height. I could see the roof and a slice of the inside of the cabin.

By this time, the schooner and her little companion were gliding pretty swiftly through the water. Indeed we were already level with the campfire. The ship was talking loudly, as sailors say. She treaded the countless ripples with an **incessant** rolling splash.

Until I got my eye above the window edge, I couldn't understand why the watchmen had taken no alarm. However, one glance was enough. And it was only one glance that I dared take from that unsteady skiff. It showed me Hands and his companion locked together in deadly wrestle. Each had a hand upon the other's throat.

I dropped into the coracle again, and none too soon, for I was nearly overboard. I could see nothing for the moment but these two furious, reddened faces. They were swaying together under the smoky lamp. I shut my eyes to let them grow once more familiar with the darkness.

The endless melody had come to an end at last. The whole diminished company about the campfire had broken into the chorus I had heard so often:

"Fifteen men on the dead man's chest—
 Yo-ho-ho, and a bottle of rum!
Drink and the devil had done for the rest—
 Yo-ho-ho, and a bottle of rum!"

I thought about how busy drink and the devil were at that very moment in the cabin of the *Hispaniola*. Then I was surprised by a sudden lurch of the coracle. At the same moment, she turned sharply and seemed to change her course. The speed had greatly increased in the meantime.

I opened my eyes at once. All around me were little ripples. They combed over with a sharp bristling sound and they were slightly phosphorescent.[2] I was still being whirled along a few yards in the wake of the schooner.

The *Hispaniola* herself seemed to change her course. I saw her spars toss a little against the blackness of the night. Nay, as I looked longer, I was sure she also was wheeling to the southward.

I glanced over my shoulder and my heart jumped against my ribs. There—right behind me—was the glow of the campfire. The current had turned at right angles. It was sweeping the tall schooner and the little dancing coracle around along with it. Ever quickening, ever bubbling higher, ever muttering louder, it went spinning through the narrows for the open sea.

Suddenly the schooner gave a violent turn in front of me. She turned through twenty degrees, perhaps. Almost at the same moment, one shout followed another from on board. I could hear feet pounding on the companion ladder. I knew that the two drunkards had at last been interrupted in their quarrel. They had been awakened to a sense of their disaster.

I lay down flat in the bottom of that wretched coracle and devoutly recommended my spirit to its Maker.[3] At the end of the straits, I was sure we'd run into some bar of raging breakers.[4] Then all my troubles would be ended speedily. Though I could perhaps bear to die, I couldn't bear to look upon my fate as it approached.

---

[2] Something that naturally gives off light is phosphorescent. The ocean sometimes looks as if it's glowing because of many small, shiny jellyfish.

[3] Jim is praying to go to heaven if he is killed.

[4] Straits are narrow bodies of water that connect two larger bodies of water. A bar of raging breakers is a group of rough waves that break into foam.

So I must have lain for hours. The coracle was constantly beaten to and fro upon the rolling waves. Now and again I was wetted with flying sprays. And I never ceased to expect death at the next plunge.

Gradually weariness grew upon me. A numbness, an occasional **stupor,** fell upon my mind even in the midst of my terrors. Sleep at last came unexpectedly. In my sea-tossed coracle I lay and dreamed of home and the old "Admiral Benbow."

Chapter 24 (Summary)

The Cruise of the Coracle

It was broad daylight when Jim awoke. He found the coracle tossing about at the southwest end of Treasure Island. The sun was coming up behind the Spy-glass. The nearby shore was very rocky and edged with high cliffs.

The current carried the small coracle into the sea. Fortunately, the waves weren't too rough and the coracle remained afloat. However, whenever Jim sat up to paddle or tried to change course, the boat threatened to overturn. He lay in the bottom for a long time, wondering if he'd ever reach land.

Jim began to feel frightened, but he kept calm. He used his cap to empty the little boat of water. Finally, he realized that he could paddle if he kept his weight very low in the coracle. He began to make slow progress back toward the island. He could see that he was going to miss the point called Cape of the Woods. But he had hopes of landing on the next point of land beyond that.

The sun was hot, and thirst was burning Jim's throat. The sight of the nearby trees made him long for land. But then he saw something that made him change his plans. The *Hispaniola* was less than half a mile in front of him.

The schooner's mainsail and two jibs were up and filled with the breeze. As Jim watched, the big ship changed direction. Then she turned and stood facing the wind, her sails flapping uselessly. Again and again, the schooner started off in a new direction. Then it turned into the wind and stopped.

Jim thought that the seamen on board must be drunk. It was clear that nobody was steering the schooner. Jim figured that if he could get on board, maybe he could return the ship to the captain.

He finally caught up with the wandering ship. He

leaped for the schooner and caught onto the bowsprit—the metal piece that sticks out of the front of the ship. The schooner ran over the coracle and sank it. And Jim was left hanging on the bowsprit. He realized he now had no way of getting back to the island.

Chapter 25

I Strike the Jolly Roger

Vocabulary Preview

The following words appear in this chapter. Review the list and get to know the words before you read the chapter.

elated—overjoyed; delighted
foraging—searching; hunting
idle—quiet; still
infernal—dreadful; horrible
sidling—moving sideways

I had barely gained a position on the bowsprit when the flying jib flapped and the schooner began to turn. The sound was like the report of a gun. The schooner trembled as she reversed her direction. But the next moment—the other sails still drawing wind—the jib flapped back again and hung **idle.**

This had nearly tossed me off into the sea. Now I lost no time. I crawled back along the bowsprit and tumbled headfirst on the deck.

I was on the lee side of the forecastle. The mainsail was still drawing. It hid a certain portion of the afterdeck from me. Not a soul was to be seen. The planks, which had not been mopped since the mutiny, bore the prints of many feet. An empty bottle that was broken by the neck tumbled to and fro like a live thing.

Suddenly the *Hispaniola* came right into the wind. The jibs behind me cracked aloud. The rudder slammed to. The whole ship gave a sickening heave and shudder.

At the same moment, the main boom swung inboard and the sheet groaned in the blocks. I now saw the lee afterdeck.

There were the two watchmen, sure enough. Red-cap was on his back, as stiff as a handspike.[1] His arms were stretched out like those of a crucifix. His teeth showed through his open lips. Israel Hands was propped against the bulwarks. His chin was on his chest and his hands were lying open before him on the deck. His face was as white under its tan as a tallow candle.

For a while the ship kept bucking and **sidling** like a vicious horse. The sails filled, now on one tack, now on another. The boom swung to and fro till the mast groaned aloud under the strain. Now and again, too, there would come a cloud of light spray over the bulwark and a heavy blow of the ship's bows against the swell. This great rigged ship fought the water with much more violence than my homemade, lopsided coracle, now gone to the bottom of the sea.

At every jump of the schooner, Red-cap slipped to and fro. But—what was ghastly to behold—neither his attitude nor his unmoving, teeth-disclosing grin was in any way disturbed by this rough treatment. At every jump, too, Hands appeared still more to sink into himself and settle down upon the deck. His feet slid ever the farther out, and his whole body sloped towards the stern. Little by little, his face became hidden from me. At last, I could see nothing beyond his ear and the frayed ringlet of one whisker.

At the same time, I noticed splashes of dark blood on the planks around both of them. I began to feel sure that they had killed each other in their drunken fury.

Thus I stood looking and wondering. In a calm moment the ship became still, and Israel Hands turned partly around. With a low moan, he squirmed back to the position in which I had seen him first. The moan told of pain and deadly weakness. And the way in which his jaw

---

[1] A handspike is a bar used as a lever.

hung open went right to my heart. But when I remembered the talk I had overheard from the apple barrel, all pity left me.

I walked aft until I reached the mainmast.

"Come aboard, Mr. Hands," I said with scorn.

He rolled his eyes round heavily, but he was too far gone to express surprise. All he could do was to utter one word, "Brandy."

It occurred to me there was no time to lose. Dodging the boom as it once more lurched across the deck, I slipped aft. I went down the companion stairs into the cabin.

It was such a scene of confusion as you can hardly imagine. All the lock-fast places had been broken open in quest of the chart. The floor was thick with mud, where pirates had sat down to drink or talk things over after wading in the marshes round their camp. The bulkheads—all painted in clear white and beaded round with gold plating—bore a pattern of dirty hands.

Dozens of empty bottles clinked together in corners to the rolling of the ship. One of the doctor's medical books lay open on the table. Half the pages were torn out of it. I suppose they were used for pipe lights. In the midst of all this, the lamp still cast a smoky glow, dim and brown as umber.[2]

I went into the cellar. All the barrels were gone. Of the bottles, a most surprising number had been drunk out and thrown away. Certainly not a man of them could ever have been sober since the mutiny began.

Foraging about, I found a bottle with some brandy left, for Hands. For myself I routed out some biscuit, some pickled fruits, a great bunch of raisins, and a piece of cheese. With these I came on deck.

I put my own stock behind the rudder head and well out of the coxswain's reach. I went forward to the water-breaker and had a good deep drink of water. Then—and not till then—I gave Hands the brandy.

[2] Umber is dark brownish-yellow earth.

He must have drunk a gill[3] before he took the bottle from his mouth.

"Aye," said he, "by thunder but I wanted some o' that!"

I had sat down already in my own corner and begun to eat.

"Much hurt?" I asked him.

He grunted, or barked, I might rather say.

"If that doctor was aboard," he said, "I'd be right enough in a couple of turns. But I don't have no manner of luck, you see. That's what's the matter with me. As for that swab, he's good as dead, he is," he added. He meant the man with the red cap. "He wasn't no seaman, anyhow. And where might you have come from?"

"Well," said I, "I've come aboard to take possession of this ship, Mr. Hands. You'll please regard me as your captain until further notice."

He looked at me sourly enough, but said nothing. Some of the color had come back into his cheeks, though he still looked very sick. He still continued to slip out and settle down as the ship banged about.

"By-the-by," I continued, "I can't have these colors, Mr. Hands. By your leave, I'll take them down. Better none than these."

And I ran to the color lines, again dodging the boom. I handed down their cursed black flag and chucked it overboard.

"God save the king!" said I, waving my cap. "And there's an end to Captain Silver!"

He watched me sharply and slyly, his chin all the while on his breast.

"I reckon," he said at last, "I reckon, Cap'n Hawkins, you'll kind of want to get ashore now. S'pose we talks."

"Why yes," said I, "with all my heart, Mr. Hands. Say on." And I went back to my meal with a good appetite.

"This man," he began, nodding weakly at the corpse. "O'Brien were his name—a rank Irelander—this man

---

[3] The British gill is a unit of measure equal to five fluid ounces.

and me got the canvas on her. We meant to sail her back. Well, *he's* dead now, he is—as dead as bilge. Who's to sail this ship, I don't see. Unless I gives you a hint, you ain't that man as far's I can tell.

"Now look here," Hands went on. "You give me food and drink and an old scarf or handkerchief to tie my wound up, you do. And I'll tell you how to sail her. That's about square all round, I take it."

"I'll tell you one thing," says I. "I'm not going back to Captain Kidd's anchorage. I meant to get into North Inlet and beach her quietly there."

"To be sure you did," he cried. "Why, I ain't such an **infernal** lubber, after all. I can see, can't I? I've tried my fling, I have, and I've lost. It's you who has the wind of me. North Inlet? Why I haven't no choice, not I! I'd help you sail her up to Execution Dock, by thunder! So I would."

Well, there was some sense in this, it seemed to me. We struck our bargain on the spot. In three minutes I had the *Hispaniola* sailing easily before the wind along the coast of Treasure Island. I had good hopes of turning the northern point before noon and beating down again as far as North Inlet before high water. Then we might beach her safely and wait until the ebbing tide permitted us to land.

Then I lashed the tiller and went below to my own chest. I got a soft silk handkerchief of my mother's. With this, and with my aid, Hands bound up the great bleeding stab he had received in the thigh. After he had eaten a little and had a swallow or two more of the brandy, he began to pick up noticeably. He sat up straighter, spoke louder and clearer, and looked in every way like another man.

The breeze served us superbly. We skimmed before it like a bird. The coast of the island flashed by and the view changed every minute. Soon we were past the high lands and bowling beside low, sandy country sparsely dotted with dwarf pines. Soon we were beyond that again and had turned the corner of the rocky hill that ends the island on the north.

I was greatly **elated** with my new command. And I was pleased with the bright sunshiny weather and these different views of the coast. I had now plenty of water and good things to eat. My conscience—which had attacked me hard for my desertion—was quieted by the great conquest I had made.

I think I should have had nothing left me to desire if it wasn't for the coxswain. His eyes followed me derisively about the deck. And an odd smile appeared constantly on his face. It was a smile that had something in it both of pain and weakness—a weary old man's smile. But besides that there was a grain of mockery. There was a shadow of trickery in his expression as he slyly watched, and watched, and watched me at my work.

Chapter 26

Israel Hands

Vocabulary Preview

The following words appear in this chapter. Review the list and get to know the words before you read the chapter.

inclination—desire; wish
perplexity—confusion; puzzlement
pretext—excuse; cover-up
solemnity—seriousness
subordinate—junior; one who ranks below another
volition—free will; choice

The wind—serving us just as we desired—now hauled into the west. We could run so much the easier from the northeast corner of the island to the mouth of the North Inlet. Only we had no power to anchor. And we dared not beach her till the tide had flowed a good deal farther. So time hung on our hands.

The coxswain told me how to lay the ship to. After a good many tries, I succeeded. We both sat in silence over another meal.

"Cap'n," said he, finally, with that same uncomfortable smile. "Here's my old shipmate, O'Brien. Suppose you was to heave him overboard. I ain't particular as a rule. And I don't take no blame for settling his hash. But I don't reckon him ornamental, now, do you?"

"I'm not strong enough and I don't like the job. There

he lies, for me," said I.

"This here's an unlucky ship—this *Hispaniola,* Jim," Hands went on, blinking. "There's a power o' men been killed in this *Hispaniola.* A sight o' poor seamen dead and gone since you and me took ship at Bristol. I never seed such dirty luck, not I. There was this here O'Brien, now—he's dead, ain't he? Well, now, I'm no scholar. And you're a lad who can read and figure. To put it straight, do you take it as a dead man is dead for good? Or do he come alive again?"

"You can kill the body, Mr. Hands, but not the spirit. You must know that already," I replied. "O'Brien there is in another world and maybe watching us."

"Ah!" says he. "Well, that's unfortunate—appears as if killing parties was a waste of time. However, spirits don't reckon for much, by what I've seen. I'll chance it with the spirits, Jim. And now, you've spoke up free. And I'll take it kind if you'd step down into that there cabin and get me a—well, a—shiver my timbers! I can't hit the name on it. Well, you get me a bottle of wine, Jim. This here brandy's too strong for my head."

Now, the coxswain's hesitation seemed to be unnatural. And as for the idea of his preferring wine to brandy, I entirely disbelieved it. The whole story was a **pretext.** He wanted me to leave the deck—so much was plain. But with what purpose I could in no way imagine.

His eyes never met mine. They kept wandering to and fro, up and down. Now they moved with a look to the sky, now with a flitting glance upon the dead O'Brien. All the time he kept smiling and putting his tongue out in the most guilty, embarrassed manner. A child could have told that he was bent on some deception.

However, I was prompt with my answer, for I saw where my advantage lay. With a fellow so densely stupid, I could easily hide my suspicions to the end.

"Some wine?" I said. "Far better. Will you have white or red?"

"Well, I reckon it's about the blessed same to me,

shipmate," he replied. "As long as it's strong and there's plenty of it, what's the difference?"

"All right," I answered. "I'll bring you port,[1] Mr. Hands. But I'll have to dig for it."

With that, I scuttled down the companion with all the noise I could. I slipped off my shoes and ran quietly along the galley. I mounted the forecastle ladder and popped my head out of the fore companion. I knew Hands wouldn't expect to see me there. Yet I took every precaution possible. And certainly the worst of my suspicions proved too true.

Hands had risen from his position to the hands and knees. His leg obviously hurt him pretty sharply when he moved, for I could hear him stifle a groan. Yet it was at a good rattling rate that he dragged himself across the deck. In half a minute, he had reached the scuppers.

The coxswain picked a long knife, or rather a short dirk,[2] out of a coil of rope. It was discolored up to the hilt with blood. He looked upon it for a moment, thrusting forth his under-jaw. He tried the point upon his hand. Then—hastily concealing it in the bosom of his jacket— he rolled back again to his old place against the bulwark.

This was all that I required to know. Israel could move about and he was now armed. If he had been at so much trouble to get rid of me, it was plain that I was meant to be the victim. What he would do afterwards was more than I could say, of course. Would he try to crawl right across the island from North Inlet to the camp among the swamps? Or would he fire Long Tom,[3] trusting his own comrades might come first to help him?

Yet I felt sure that I could trust him in one point, since in that our interests jumped together. That was in what would be done with the schooner. We both desired to have her stranded safe enough in a sheltered place. And when the time came, we wanted her to be got off

---

[1] Port is a sweet wine, usually made in Portugal.
[2] A dirk is a type of dagger—a short, pointed weapon.
[3] Long Tom was a gun on the ship, probably the one the pirates fired earlier.

again with as little labor and danger as might be. Until that was done, I considered that my life would certainly be spared.

While I was thus turning the business over in my mind, I hadn't been idle with my body. I had stolen back to the cabin and slipped once more into my shoes. I laid my hand at random on a bottle of wine. With this for an excuse, I now made my reappearance on the deck.

Hands lay as I had left him, all fallen together in a bundle. His eyelids were lowered, as though he was too weak to bear the light. However, he looked up at my coming. He knocked the neck off the bottle like a man who had done the same thing often. He took a good swig with his favorite toast of "Here's luck!" Then he lay quiet for a little. And then he pulled out a stick of tobacco and begged me to cut him a quid.

"Cut me a junk o' that," says he. "I haven't no knife, and barely strength enough if I had. Ah, Jim, Jim, I reckon I've missed stays![4] Cut me a quid, as it'll likely be the last, lad. I'm going to my long home, and no mistake."

"Well," said I, "I'll cut you some tobacco. But if I was you and thought myself so bad off, I'd go to my prayers like a Christian man."

"Why?" said he. "Now you tell me why."

"Why?" I cried. "You were asking me just now about the dead. You've broken your trust. You've lived in sin and lies and blood. There's a man you killed lying at your feet this moment. And you ask me why! For God's mercy, Mr. Hands, that's why."

I spoke with a little heat. I was thinking of the bloody dirk he had hidden in his pocket—the one which he planned in his ill thoughts to end me with. For his part, he took a great swallow of the wine. He spoke with the most unusual **solemnity.**

"For thirty years," he said, "I've sailed the seas. I've seen good and bad, better and worse, fair weather and

---

[4] *In stays* refers to changing a ship's direction, or tacking. Hands indicates that he might have missed some chances in life.

foul. I've seen supplies running out, knives going, and what not. Well, now I tell you, I never seen good come o' goodness yet. Him that strikes first is my fancy. Dead men don't bite. Them's my views—amen, so be it.

"And now you look here," he added, suddenly changing his tone. "We've had about enough of this foolery. The tide's made good enough by now. You just take my orders, Cap'n Hawkins, and we'll sail slap in and be done with it."

All told, we had barely two miles to run. But the navigation was tricky. The entrance to this northern anchorage wasn't only narrow and shallow, but lay east and west. The schooner must be nicely handled to be got in. I think I was a good, prompt **subordinate,** and I'm very sure that Hands was an excellent pilot. We went about and about and dodged in, shaving the banks. The ship moved with a confidence and a neatness that was a pleasure to behold.

We had barely passed the heads before the land closed around us. The shores of North Inlet were as thickly wooded as those of the southern anchorage. But the space was longer and narrower and more like what it really was—the estuary[5] of a river.

Right before us at the southern end, we saw the wreck of a ship in the last stages of decay. It had been a great vessel of three masts. But it had lain long exposed to the injuries of the weather. It was hung about with great webs of dripping seaweed. On the deck of it, shore bushes had taken root and now flourished thick with flowers. It was a sad sight, but it showed us that the anchorage was calm.

"Now," said Hands, "look there. There's a good spot for to beach a ship in. Fine, flat sand, never a catspaw, trees all around of it, and flowers a-blowing like a garden on that old ship."

"And once beached," I inquired, "how shall we get her off again?"

[5] An estuary is the place where the current of a river meets the tides of the sea.

"Why so," he replied. "You take a line ashore there on the other side at low water. Take a turn about one o' them big pines. Bring the line back and take a turn around the capstan and lie to for the tide. Come high water, all hands take a pull upon the line and off she comes as sweet as nature. And now, boy, you stand by. We're nearer the spot now and she's moving too fast. Starboard a little—so—steady—starboard—larboard a little—steady—steady!"

So he gave his commands. I breathlessly obeyed them till he cried all of a sudden, "Now, my hearty, luff!" And I put the helm hard up, and the *Hispaniola* swung round rapidly and ran headfirst for the low wooded shore.

The excitement of these last maneuvers had somewhat interfered with the sharp watch I had kept on the coxswain. Even then, I was still so much interested in waiting for the ship to touch that I had quite forgot the danger that hung over my head. I stood leaning over the starboard bulwarks and watching the ripples spreading wide before the bows.

I might have fallen without a struggle for my life. But a certain uneasiness seized upon me and made me turn my head. Perhaps I had heard a creak or seen his shadow moving with the tail of my eye. Perhaps it was an instinct like a cat's. But sure enough, when I looked round there was Hands already halfway toward me. The dirk was in his right hand.

We must both have cried out aloud when our eyes met. Mine was the shrill cry of terror. His was a roar of fury like a charging bull's. At the same instant, he threw himself forward and I leapt sideways toward the bow. As I did so, I let go of the tiller, which sprang sharp to leeward. I think this saved my life, for it struck Hands across the chest and stopped him—for the moment—dead.

Before he could recover, I was safe out of the corner where he had me trapped. Now I had all the deck to dodge about. Just forward of the mainmast, I stopped and drew a pistol from my pocket. I took a cool aim, although he had already turned and was once more coming directly at me. I drew the trigger.

The hammer fell, but there followed neither flash nor sound. The priming[6] was useless with sea water. I cursed myself for my neglect. Why hadn't I long before reprimed and reloaded my only weapons? Then I wouldn't have been a mere fleeing sheep before this butcher, as I was now.

Wounded as Hands was, it was wonderful how fast he could move. His gray-streaked hair tumbled over his face. His face itself was as red as a red flag with his haste and fury. I had no time to try my other pistol. Nor indeed did I have much **inclination.** I was sure it would be useless.

One thing I saw plainly—I must not simply retreat before him. Otherwise he would speedily have me boxed into the bows just as he had so nearly boxed me in the stern a moment before. Once I was so caught, nine or ten inches of the bloodstained dirk would be my last experience on this side of eternity. I placed my palms against the mainmast—which was of a goodish bigness— and waited. Every nerve was stretched to the limit.

Seeing that I meant to dodge, he also paused. A moment or two passed with fake moves on his part and corresponding movements on mine. It was such a game as I had often played at home about the rocks of Black Hill Cove. But never before with such a wildly beating heart as now, you may be sure.

Still, as I say, it was a boy's game. I thought I could hold my own at it against an elderly seaman with a wounded leg. Indeed, my courage had begun to rise so high that I allowed myself a few hurried thoughts on how the affair would end. I saw that I could certainly spin it out for long. But I saw no hope of any ultimate escape.

Well, while things stood thus, suddenly the *Hispaniola* struck, staggered, and ground for an instant in the sand. Then, swift as a blow, she tilted over till the deck stood at

[6] Priming is the explosive that was used in guns at that time.

an angle of forty-five degrees. About a puncheon of water splashed into the scupper holes. It lay in a pool between the deck and bulwark.

We were both of us capsized in a second. Both of us rolled almost together into the scuppers. The dead red-cap tumbled stiffly after us with his arms still spread out. Indeed, we were all so near that my head came against the coxswain's foot with a crack that made my teeth rattle. Blow and all, I was the first on my feet again, for Hands had got tangled up with the dead body.

The sudden tilting of the ship had made the deck no place for running on. I had to find some new way of escape and right away. My foe was now almost touching me. Quick as thought, I sprang into the mizzen shrouds. I rattled up hand over hand and didn't draw a breath till I was seated on the cross-trees.

I had been saved by being prompt. The dirk had struck not half a foot below me as I continued my upward flight. There stood Israel Hands, with his mouth open and his face upturned to mine. He was a perfect statue of surprise and disappointment.

Now that I had a moment to myself, I lost no time in changing the priming of my pistol. Then I had one ready for service. And to make safety doubly sure, I went on to draw the load of the other. I recharged it afresh from the beginning.

My new employment struck Hands all of a heap. He began to see the dice going against him. After an obvious hesitation, he also hauled himself heavily into the shrouds. With the dirk in his teeth, he began slowly and painfully to mount.

It cost him no end of time and groans to haul his wounded leg behind him. I had quietly finished my arrangements before he was much more than a third of the way up. Then—with a pistol in either hand—I addressed him.

"One more step, Mr. Hands," said I, "and I'll blow your brains out! Dead men don't bite, you know," I added, with a chuckle.

He stopped instantly. I could see by the movement of his face that he was trying to think. The process was so slow and difficult that I laughed aloud in my new-found security. At last, with a swallow or two, he spoke. His face still wore the same expression of extreme **perplexity.** In order to speak, he had to take the dagger from his mouth. But in all else he remained unmoved.

"Jim," says he, "I reckon we're in a mess, you and me. I'd have had you but for that there lurch. But I don't have no luck, not I. I reckon I'll have to give up. That comes hard for a master mariner to a ship's younker like you, Jim. You see?"

I was drinking in his words and smiling away, as proud as a cock upon a wall. Then, all in a breath, back went Hands' right hand over his shoulder. Something sang like an arrow through the air. I felt a blow and then a sharp pang. And there I was, pinned by the shoulder to the mast.

In the horrible pain and surprise of the moment, both my pistols went off. I can hardly say it was by my own **volition,** and I'm sure it was without a conscious aim. Both pistols escaped out of my hands. They didn't fall alone. With a choked cry, the coxswain loosed his grasp upon the shrouds and plunged headfirst into the water.

Chapter 27 (Summary)

"Pieces of Eight"

Because the schooner was leaning far over, Jim was hanging out over the water. He could see Israel Hands' body sink into the water, never to rise again. Jim began to feel sick, faint, and terrified. He was still pinned to the mast with the dirk. His shoulder burned like a hot iron. Blood ran down his back and chest.

Thinking about pulling out the knife, Jim shuddered. That shudder tore away the little pinch of skin that the knife held. Though he bled more, Jim was now tacked to the mast only by his coat and shirt. A sudden jerk broke him free, and he climbed down to the deck of the ship.

Jim went below deck and did what he could to patch up his wound. It was still bleeding, but it was neither deep nor dangerous. Going back up on deck, he heaved the corpse of O'Brien overboard. The two dead pirates lay side by side in the water.

Jim was now alone on the ship. He was worried about the leaning ship going under. So he took down the jibs. He had to cut the lines to get the mainsail down. The canvas of the mainsail floated in the water.

Jim noticed the water seemed fairly shallow. He jumped in and found it was waist-deep. He happily waded ashore. By this time, the sun was going down.

When he reached land, Jim set off to rejoin his companions in the blockhouse. He was proud of himself for freeing the schooner of the mutineers. He felt Captain Smollett and the others would forgive him for his desertion.

The night grew dark, but then the moon rose. With that light, Jim moved quickly back toward the stockade. When he got there, he could see the embers of a huge bonfire. But he could see no one, not even a guard. He felt that something had gone wrong.

Jim crept over the stockade fence. He was relieved when he heard someone snoring, and he walked into the blockhouse. His foot struck the leg of a sleeper, who groaned but didn't wake up. Then a shrill voice broke the silence, screaming, "Pieces of eight! Pieces of eight! Pieces of eight! Pieces of eight!"

It was Silver's parrot, Captain Flint! The sleepers woke and jumped up. Jim tried to run, but he bumped into someone who held him tightly. Long John Silver's voice ordered someone to bring a torch.

PART VI: CAPTAIN SILVER

Chapter 28

In the Enemy's Camp

Vocabulary Preview

The following words appear in this chapter. Review the list and get to know the words before you read the chapter.

apprehensions—fears; worries
composure—self-control; calmness
despair—hopelessness; gloom
incensed—furious; very angry
perished—died
preening—grooming; smoothing
unruly—out of control; disorderly

The red glare of the torch lit up the inside of the blockhouse. I found the worst of my **apprehensions** were realized. The pirates were in possession of the house and stores. There was the cask of cognac, there were the pork and bread, as before. And—what increased my horror tenfold—there wasn't a sign of any prisoner. I could only judge that all had **perished.** My heart hurt me sorely because I hadn't been there to perish with them.

There were six of the buccaneers, all told. Not another man was left alive. Five of them were on their feet, flushed and swollen. They'd been suddenly called out of the first sleep of drunkenness.

The sixth man had only risen upon his elbow. He was deadly pale. And the bloodstained bandage round his head told that he had recently been wounded and still more recently dressed.[1] I remembered the man who had been shot and had run back among the woods in the great attack. I didn't doubt that this was he.

The parrot sat **preening** her feathers on Long John's shoulder. I thought Silver himself looked somewhat paler and more stern than I was used to. He still wore the fine broadcloth suit in which he had fulfilled his mission. But it was bitterly the worse for wear. It was smeared with clay and torn with the sharp twigs and thorns of the woods.

"So," said he, "here's Jim Hawkins, shiver my timbers! Dropped in, like, eh? Well, come, I take that friendly."

And with that, he sat down across the brandy cask and began to fill a pipe.

"Give me a loan of the link, Dick," said he. Then, when he had a good light, he added, "That'll do, lad. Stick the light in the wood heap. And you, gentlemen, bring yourselves to! You needn't stand up for Mr. Hawkins. *He'll* excuse you, you may lay to that.

"And so, Jim" he went on, stopping the tobacco. "Here you were, and quite a pleasant surprise for poor old John. I could see you were smart when first I set my eyes on you. But this here gets away from me clean, it do."

As may be well supposed, I made no answer to all this. They had set me with my back against the wall. I stood there, looking Silver in the face. My expression was brave enough to all outward appearance, I hoped. But black **despair** was in my heart.

Silver took a whiff or two of his pipe with great **composure,** and then ran on again.

"Now you see, Jim, so be as you *are* here," says he, "I'll give you a piece of my mind. I've always liked you, I have. For you're a lad of spirit and the picture of my own self when I was young and handsome. I always wanted

---

[1] *Dressed* means "bandaged."

you to join and take your share and die a gentleman. And now, my proud one, you've got to. Cap'n Smollett's a fine seaman, as I'll own up to any day. But he's stiff on discipline.

" 'Duty is duty,' says Cap'n Smollett, and right he is. Just you keep clear of the cap'n. The doctor himself is gone dead against you—'ungrateful scamp' was what he said. The short and the long of the whole story is about here. You can't go back to your own lot, for they won't have you. Unless you start a third ship's company all by yourself, which might be lonely, you'll have to join with Cap'n Silver."

So far so good. My friends were still alive, then. I partly believed the truth of Silver's statement, that the cabin party were **incensed** at me for my desertion. But I was more relieved than distressed by what I heard.

"I don't say nothing as to your being in our hands," continued Silver. "Though there you are and you may lay to it. I'm all for argument. I never seen good come out o' threatening. If you like the service, well, you'll join. And if you don't, Jim, why, you're free to answer no—free and welcome, shipmate. If fairer can be said by a mortal seaman, shiver my sides!"

"Am I to answer, then?" I asked, with a very shaky voice. Through all this sneering talk, I was made to feel the threat of death that overhung me. My cheeks burned and my heart beat painfully in my breast.

"Lad," said Silver, "no one's a-pressing of you. Take your bearings. None of us won't hurry you, mate. Time goes so pleasant in your company, you see."

"Well," says I, growing a bit bolder, "if I'm to choose, I declare I have a right to know what's what. Why you're here and where my friends are."

"Wot's wot?" repeated one of the buccaneers in a deep growl. "Ah, he'd be a lucky one as knowed that!"

"Perhaps you'll batten down your hatches[2] till you're spoke to, my friend," cried Silver savagely to this speaker.

---

[2] *Batten down your hatches* means "keep quiet."

And then he replied to me in his first gracious tones. "Mr. Hawkins," said he, "yesterday morning in the dog watch, down came Doctor Livesey with a flag of truce. Says he, 'Cap'n Silver, you're sold out. Ship's gone.'

"Well, maybe we'd been taking a glass and a song to help it round. I won't say no. At least none of us had looked out at the ship. We looked out then and, by thunder! The old ship was gone. I never seen a pack o' fools look fishier. And you may lay to that if I tells you that looked the fishiest. 'Well,' says the doctor, 'let's bargain.'

"We bargained, him and I, and here we are. Stores, brandy, blockhouse, and the firewood you was thoughtful enough to cut. In a manner of speaking, we have the whole blessed boat from top to bottom. As for them, they've tramped. I don't know where's they are."

He drew again quietly at his pipe.

"And," he went on, "unless you should take it into that head of yours that you was included in the treaty, here's the last word that was said. 'How many are you to leave?' says I. 'Four,' says he. 'Four, and one of us wounded. As for that boy, I don't know where he is, confound him,' says he. 'Nor I don't much care. We're about sick of him.' These was his words."

"Is that all?" I asked.

"Well, it's all that you're to hear, my son," replied Silver.

"And now I'm to choose?"

"And now you're to choose, and you may lay to that," said Silver.

"Well," said I, "I'm not such a fool but I know pretty well what I have to look for. Let the worst come to the worst, it's little I care. I've seen too many die since I fell in with you. But there's a thing or two I have to tell you," I said. And by this time I was quite excited.

"The first is this: here you are in a bad way—ship lost, treasure lost, men lost. Your whole business is gone to wreck. If you want to know who did it—it was I! I was in the apple barrel the night we sighted land. I heard you, John, and you, Dick Johnson, and Hands, who's now at the bottom of the sea. I told every word you said before the hour was out.

"And as for the schooner," said I, "it was I who cut her cable. And it was I that killed the men you had aboard of her. And it was I who brought her where you'll never see her more, not one of you. The laugh's on my side. I've had the top of this business from the first.

"I don't fear you any more than I fear a fly," I went on. "Kill me, if you please, or spare me. But one thing I'll say and no more. If you spare me, bygones are bygones. When you fellows are in court for piracy, I'll save you all I can. It's for you to choose. Kill another and do yourselves no good. Or spare me and keep a witness to save you from the gallows."

I stopped, for I was out of breath, I tell you. To my wonder, not a man of them moved. They all sat staring at me like as many sheep. And while they were still staring, I broke out again.

"And now, Mr. Silver," I said, "I believe you're the best man here. If things go the worst, I'll take it kind of you to let the doctor know the way I took it."

"I'll bear it in mind," said Silver, with an odd accent. For the life of me, I couldn't decide whether he was laughing at my request or had been favorably affected by my courage.

"I'll put one to that," cried the old red-faced seaman named Morgan. I'd seen him in Long John's tavern upon the quays of Bristol. "It was him that knowed Black Dog."

"Well, and see here," added the sea cook. "I'll put another again to that, by thunder! For it was this same boy that faked the chart from Billy Bones. First and last, we've split upon Jim Hawkins!"

"Then here goes!" said Morgan, with an oath.

And he sprang up, drawing his knife as if he had been twenty.

"Avast[3] there!" cried Silver. "Who are you, Tom Morgan? Maybe you thought you was cap'n here, perhaps. By the powers, but I'll teach you better! Cross me and you'll go where many a good man's gone before you, first and last, these thirty years back. Some went to the yard-arm, shiver my sides! Some went to the plank. And all went to feed the fishes. There's never a man looked me between the eyes and seen a good day afterwards, Tom Morgan. You may lay to that."

Morgan paused, but a hoarse murmur rose from the others.

"Tom's right," said one.

"I stood hazing long enough from one," added another. "I'll be hanged if I'll be hazed by you, John Silver."

"Did any of you gentlemen want to have it out with *me?*" roared Silver. He bent far forward from his position on the keg. His pipe still glowed in his right hand. "Put a name on what you're at. You ain't dumb, I reckon. Him that wants shall get it. Have I lived this many years only to have a son of a rum-puncheon cock his hat across my bow at the latter end of it?

"You know the way," Silver went on. "You're all gentlemen o' fortune, by your account. Well, I'm ready. Take a cutlass, him that dares. I'll see the color of his inside, crutch and all, before that pipe's empty."

Not a man stirred. Not a man answered.

"That's your sort, is it?" Silver added, returning his pipe to his mouth. "Well, you're a merry lot to look at, anyway. Not much worth to fight, you ain't. Perhaps you can understand King George's English. I'm cap'n here by election. I'm cap'n here because I'm the best man by a long sea mile. You won't fight as gentlemen o' fortune should. Then, by thunder, you'll obey, and you may lay to it!

"I like that boy, now," Silver continued. "I never seen a better boy than that. He's more a man than any pair of

___
[3]*Avast* means "stop" or "cease."

rats of you in this here house. What I say is this: let me see him that'll lay a hand on him—that's what I say, and you may lay to it."

There was a long pause after this. I stood straight up against the wall. My heart was still going like a sledge hammer. But there was a ray of hope now shining in my bosom. Silver leaned back against the wall, his arms crossed, his pipe in the corner of his mouth. He was as calm as though he had been in church. Yet his eye kept wandering nervously and he kept the tail of it on his **unruly** followers.

They on their part drew gradually together towards the far end of the blockhouse. The low hiss of their whispering sounded in my ear nonstop like a stream. One after another they'd look up and the red light of the torch would fall for a second on their nervous faces. But it wasn't towards me, it was towards Silver that they turned their eyes.

"You seem to have a lot to say," remarked Silver, spitting far into the air. "Pipe up and let me hear it or lay to."

"Ask your pardon, sir," returned one of the men. "You're pretty free with some of the rules. Maybe you'll kindly keep an eye upon the rest. This crew's dissatisfied. This crew don't value bullying a marlin-spike.[4] This crew has its rights like other crews, I'll make as free as that. By your own rules, I take it we can talk together. I ask your pardon, sir. And I acknowledge you to be captain at this moment. But I claim my right and steps outside for a council."[5]

This fellow was a long, ill-looking, yellow-eyed man

---

[4] A marlin-spike is a tool used to separate strands of rope.

[5] Pirates had a rough but democratic community. They chose their captains by election. Captains had very few privileges that the men didn't share. The captain was completely in charge only in time of battle. The highest authority was the council, which included every man on the ship. The council made decisions about where to sail and how to settle disagreements. Council decisions were made by a majority of votes. Much of this equality was developed because pirates hated the stern, often tyrannical, organization on naval and merchant ships.

of thirty-five. With an elaborate sea-salute, he stepped coolly towards the door and disappeared out of the house. One after the rest followed his example. Each made a salute as he passed, and each added some apology.

"According to rules," said one. "Forecastle council," said Morgan. And so all marched out with one remark or another. Silver and I were left alone with the torch.

The sea cook instantly removed his pipe.

"Now look you here, Jim Hawkins." He spoke in a steady whisper I could just barely hear. "You're within half a plank of death and—what's a long sight worse—of torture. They're going to throw me off. But mark you, I stand by you through thick and thin. I didn't mean to. No, not till you spoke up. I was about desperate to lose that much cash and be hanged into the bargain.

"But I see you was the right sort," said Silver. "I says to myself: You stand by Hawkins, John, and Hawkins'll stand by you. You're his last card, and by the living thunder, John, he's yours! Back to back, says I. You save your witness and he'll save your neck!"

I began dimly to understand.

"You mean all's lost?" I asked.

"Ay, by gum, I do!" he answered. "Ship gone, neck gone—that's the size of it. Once I looked into that bay, Jim Hawkins, and seen no schooner—well, I'm tough but I gave out. As for that lot and their council, mark me they're outright fools and cowards. I'll save your life from them, if so be as I can. But see here, Jim—tit for tat—you save Long John from swinging."

I was bewildered. It seemed a thing so hopeless he was asking—he, the old buccaneer, the ringleader throughout.

"What I can do, that I'll do," I said.

"It's a bargain!" cried Long John. "You speak up plucky and, by thunder! I've a chance."

He hobbled to the torch where it stood propped among the firewood and took a fresh light to his pipe.

"Understand me, Jim," he said, returning. "I've a head on my shoulders, I have. I'm on squire's side now. I know you've got that ship safe somewheres. How you done it, I don't know, but safe it is. I guess Hands and O'Brien turned soft. I never much believed in neither of *them*. Now you mark me. I ask no questions, nor I won't let others. I know when a game's up, I do. And I know a lad that's loyal. Ah, you that's young—you and me might have done a power of good together!"

He drew some cognac from the cask into a tin cup.

"Will you taste, messmate?" he asked. When I had refused, he said, "Well, I'll take a drain myself, Jim. I need it, for there's trouble on hand. And talking o' trouble, why did that doctor give me the chart, Jim?"

My face expressed a wonder so real that he saw the needlessness of further questions.

"Ah, well, he did, though," said Silver. "And there's something under that, no doubt. Something surely under that, Jim—bad or good."

He took another swallow of the brandy. And he shook his great fair head like a man who looks forward to the worst.

Chapter 29

The Black Spot Again

Vocabulary Preview

The following words appear in this chapter. Review the list and get to know the words before you read the chapter.

conspirators—plotters; schemers
contemptuously—scornfully; hatefully
deposed—removed from a high position or office; dethroned
emissary—messenger
grievances—complaints; protests
vehemence—fierceness; violence

The council of the buccaneers had lasted some time when one of them re-entered the house. He repeated the same salute, which seemed sort of scornful to my eyes. Then he begged for a moment's loan of the torch. Silver briefly agreed. The **emissary** departed again, leaving us together in the dark.

"There's a breeze coming, Jim," said Silver. By this time he had adopted quite a friendly and familiar tone.

I turned to the loophole nearest me and looked out. The embers of the great fire had almost burned themselves out. They now glowed so low and dimly that I understood why these **conspirators** desired a torch.

They were collected in a group about halfway down the slope to the stockade. One held the light. Another was on his knees in their midst. I saw the blade of an open knife in his hand. It shone with different colors in the moon and torchlight. The rest were all somewhat stooping, as though watching the movements of this last man. I could just make out that he had a book as well as a knife in his hand. I wondered how anything so out of place had come in their possession. Then the kneeling figure rose once more to his feet. The whole party began to move towards the house.

"Here they come," said I. I returned to my former position. It seemed beneath my dignity that they should find me watching them.

"Well, let 'em come, lad—let 'em come," said Silver, cheerfully. "I've still a shot in my locker."

The door opened and the five men stood huddled together just inside. They pushed one of their number forward. In any other circumstance it would have been comical to see how he slowly inched forward. He hesitated as he set down each foot, but he held his closed right hand in front of him.

"Step up, lad," cried Silver. "I won't eat you. Hand it over, lubber. I know the rules, I do. I won't hurt a deputation."[1]

Thus encouraged, the buccaneer stepped forth more briskly. He passed something to Silver, from hand to hand. Then he slipped yet more smartly back again to his companions.

The sea cook looked at what had been given him.

"The black spot! I thought so," he observed. "Where might you have got the paper? Why, hello! Look here now, this ain't lucky! You've gone and cut this out of a Bible. What fool's cut a Bible?"

"Ah, there!" said Morgan. "There! Wot did I say? No good'll come o' that, I said."

"Well, you've about fixed it now, among you," continued Silver. "You'll all swing now, I reckon. What soft-headed lubber had a Bible?"

"It was Dick," said one.

[1] A deputation is a group or person who represents others.

"Dick, was it? Then Dick can get to prayers," said Silver. "He's seen his slice of luck, has Dick, and you may lay to that."

But here the long man with the yellow eyes struck in.

"Stop that talk, John Silver," he said. "This crew has tipped you the black spot in full council, as in duty bound. Just you turn it over, as in duty bound, and see what's wrote there. Then you can talk."

"Thanky, George," replied the sea cook. "You always was brisk for business. You has the rules by heart, George, as I'm pleased to see. Well, what is it anyway? Ah! **'Deposed'**—that's it, is it? Very pretty wrote to be sure. Like print, I swear. Your hand o' write, George? Why, you was gettin' to be quite a leadin' man in this here crew. You'll be cap'n next, I shouldn't wonder. Just kindly give me that torch again, will you? This pipe don't draw."

"Come now," said George. "You don't fool this crew no more. You're a funny man, by your account. But you're over, now. You'll maybe step down off that barrel and help vote."

"I thought you said you knowed the rules," replied Silver, **contemptuously.** "At any rate, if you don't, I do. And I wait here—and I'm still your cap'n, mind—till you come out with your **grievances** and I reply. In the meantime, your black spot ain't worth a biscuit. After that, we'll see."

"Oh," replied George, "don't you worry none. *We're* all square, we are. First, you've made a mess of this cruise—you'll be a bold man to say no to that. Second, you let the enemy out o' this here trap for nothing. Why did they want out? I dunno; but it's pretty plain they wanted it. Third, you wouldn't let us go at them upon the march. Oh, we see through you, John Silver. You want to play booty, that's what's wrong with you. And then, fourth, there's this here boy."

"Is that all?" asked Silver quietly.

"Enough, too," retorted George. "We'll all swing and sun-dry for your bungling."

"Well, now, look here, I'll answer these four points. One after another, I'll answer 'em. I made a mess of this cruise, did I? Well, now, you all know what I wanted. And you all know if that had been done, that we'd 'a' been aboard the *Hispaniola* this night as ever was. Every man of us would be alive and fit and full of good plum pudding. And the treasure would have been in the hold of her, by thunder!

"Well, who crossed me?" Silver went on. "Who forced my hand, as was the lawful cap'n? Who tipped me the black spot the day we landed and began this dance? Ah, it's a fine dance—I'm with you there. And it looks mighty like a hornpipe[2] in a rope's end at Execution Dock by London town, it does.

"But who done it?" said Silver. "Why, it was Anderson and Hands and you, George Merry! And you're the last above board of that same bothersome crew. And you have the Davy Jones' nerve to up and stand for cap'n over me—you, that sank the lot of us! By the powers! This tops the stiffest yarn to nothing."

Silver paused, and I could see by the faces of George and his late comrades that these words hadn't been said in vain.

"That's for number one," cried the accused. He wiped the sweat from his brow, for he had been talking with a **vehemence** that shook the house. "Why I give you my word, I'm sick to speak to you. You've neither sense nor memory. I leave it to fancy where your mothers was that let you come to sea. Sea! Gentlemen o' fortune! I reckon tailors is your trade."

"Go on, John," said Morgan. "Speak up about the other points."

"Ah, the others!" replied John. "They're a nice lot, ain't they? You say this cruise is bungled. Ah! By gum, if you could understand how bad it's bungled, you'd see! We're that near the gallows that my neck's stiff with thinking on it. Maybe you've seen 'em, hanged in chains

---

[2] A hornpipe is a lively British folk dance.

with birds about 'em. Seamen point 'em out as they go down with the tide.

" 'Who's that?' says one," Silver continued. " 'That! Why, that's John Silver. I knowed him well,' says another. And you can hear the chains a-jangle as you go about and reach for the other buoy. Now, that's about where we are, every mother's son of us. All thanks to him and Hands and Anderson and other blundering fools of you.

"And if you want to know about number four and that boy, why shiver my timbers! Isn't he a hostage? Are we a-going to waste a hostage? No, not us. He might be our last chance and I shouldn't wonder. Kill the boy? Not me, mates!

"And number three?" said Silver. "Ah well, there's a deal to say to number three. Maybe you don't count it nothing to have a real college doctor come to see you every day. You, John, with your head broke? Or you, George Merry, that had the fever shakes upon you not six hours ago? Your eyes is the color of lemon peel to this same moment on the clock.

"And maybe you didn't know there was a companion ship coming, either? But there is, and not so long till then. We'll see who'll be glad to have a hostage when it comes to that.

"And as for number two and why I made a bargain. Well, you came crawling on your knees to me to make it. On your knees you came, you was that downhearted. And you'd have starved, too, if I hadn't—but that's nothing! You look there—that's why!"

And he cast down upon the floor a paper that I instantly recognized. It was none other than the chart on yellow paper with the three red crosses. It was the one I had found in the oilcloth at the bottom of the captain's chest. Why the doctor had given it to Silver was more than I could imagine.

But if it was puzzling to me, the appearance of the chart was incredible to the surviving mutineers. They leaped upon it like cats upon a mouse. It went from hand to hand, one tearing it from another. They accompanied their examination with oaths and cries and childish laughter. To hear them, you would have thought that not only were they fingering the very gold. But they were at sea with it in safety, besides.

"Yes," said one, "that's Flint sure enough. J.F., and a line below, with a clove hitch to it. So he done always."

"Mighty pretty," said George. "But how are we to get away with it, and us no ship?"

Silver suddenly sprang up, supporting himself with a hand against the wall. "Now I give you warning, George," he cried. "One more word of your sauce and I'll call you down and fight you. How are we to get away? Why, how do I know? You had ought to tell me that—you and the rest. You lost me my schooner with your interference, burn you! But not you, you can't. You ain't got the invention of a cockroach. But civil you can speak, and you shall, George Merry. You may lay to that."

"That's fair enough," said the old man, Morgan.

"Fair! I reckon so," said the sea cook. "You lost the ship. I found the treasure. Who's the better man at that? And now I resign, by thunder! Elect whom you please to be your cap'n now. I'm done with it."

"Silver!" they cried. "Barbecue forever! Barbecue for cap'n!"

"So that's the tune, is it?" cried the cook. "George, I reckon you'll have to wait another turn, friend. And lucky day for you as I'm not a revengeful man. But that was never my way. And now, shipmates, this black spot? 'Tain't much good now, is it? Dick's crossed his luck and spoiled his Bible, and that's about all."

"It'll do to kiss the book on still, won't it?" growled Dick. He was evidently uneasy at the curse he had brought upon himself.

"A Bible with a bit cut out!" replied Silver scornfully. "Not it. It don't bind no more'n a songbook."

"Don't it, though?" cried Dick, with a sort of joy. "Well, I reckon that's worth having, too."

"Here, Jim—here's a curiosity for you," said Silver. He tossed me the paper.

It was round, about the size of a crown piece.[3] One side was blank, for it had been the last leaf. The other contained a verse or two of Revelations.[4] These words among the rest struck sharply home upon my mind: "Without are dogs and murderers."

The printed side of the paper had been blackened with wood ash, which already began to come off and smudge my fingers. On the blank side had been written with the same material the one word, "Deposed." I have that curiosity beside me at this moment. But not a trace of writing now remains. There's only a single scratch such as a man might make with his thumb nail.

That was the end of the night's business. Soon after, with a drink all round, we lay down to sleep. The outside of Silver's vengeance was to put George Merry up as guard and to threaten him with death if he should prove unfaithful.

It was long before I could close an eye. Heaven knows I had enough to think about. There was the man whom I had slain that afternoon. There was my own most dangerous position. Above all, there was the remarkable game that I saw Silver now engaged upon. Silver was keeping the mutineers together with one hand. And he was grasping with the other after every means—possible and impossible—to make his peace and save his miserable life.

Silver himself slept peacefully and snored aloud. Yet my heart was sore for him, wicked as he was. It was sore to think on the dark dangers that surrounded and the shameful gallows that awaited him.

---

[3] A crown is a British coin.
[4] Revelations is a book in the Bible.

Chapter 30 (Summary)

On Parole

Those in the blockhouse were all wakened by a call from the woods. It was Dr. Livesey. Jim was glad to hear the doctor's voice, but he was ashamed to face him. Jim was embarrassed about sneaking away and allowing himself to be caught.

Silver greeted the doctor and told him that they had a new boarder—Jim. Dr. Livesey seemed a little disturbed by this news but didn't say anything. He came in and treated the patients among the pirates. He remarked that the pirates didn't know how to take care of themselves. They had camped in a swamp, and now they had malaria[1] in their systems.

Then Dr. Livesey asked to talk to Jim alone. George Merry and the other pirates objected, but Silver agreed. But first Silver asked Jim to give his word not to run away. Jim gave his pledge of honor.

The other mutineers accused Silver of playing both sides. They charged that he was trying to keep peace with the doctor for his own selfish interest. It was obvious to Jim that these accusations against Silver were true. Even so, Silver managed to calm the men down.

The doctor was put outside the stockade and Jim stayed inside, but they could talk privately through the fence. Dr. Livesey said that Jim had been cowardly to run off when Captain Smollett was ill. Jim began to cry, saying that he had blamed himself enough. He said that he'd be dead by now if Silver hadn't stood up for him, and it might come to that, anyhow. But what he was most afraid of was torture.

At that, Dr. Livesey urged Jim to jump the fence and run. But Jim refused to break his word. However, he told

[1] Malaria is an infectious disease carried by mosquitoes. It causes cycles of chills, fever, and sweating.

the doctor that he was afraid that if the pirates tortured him, he would tell where the ship was hidden. He described how he had gotten the ship into the North Inlet.

The doctor commented on how it was Jim who saved their lives, every time. Jim had first discovered the mutineers' plot and had found Ben Gunn. Jim had also saved the ship. Now Dr. Livesey was worried about Jim's own life.

Speaking of Ben Gunn reminded the doctor of something. He called Silver over and told him not to be in a rush to look for the treasure.

At this, Silver wondered about the actions of the doctor and his comrades. He asked the doctor to tell why he had handed over the treasure map.

Dr. Livesey refused to say more, as it wasn't his secret to tell. However, he promised he would do what he could to save Silver's life, if they all got out alive. He told Silver to keep the boy close to him and to call for help when he needed it. Then Dr. Livesey departed into the woods.

Chapter 31

The Treasure Hunt—Flint's Pointer

Vocabulary Preview

The following words appear in this chapter. Review the list and get to know the words before you read the chapter.

cunning—sly; clever
disarray—lack of order; untidiness
feasible—workable; sensible
principal—main; major
prolonged—drawn out; extended
subsist—survive; stay alive
tethered—tied; attached

Jim," said Silver, when we were alone. "If I saved your life you saved mine, and I'll not forget it. I seen the doctor waving you to run for it—with the tail of my eye, I did. And I seen you say no, as plain as hearing. Jim, that's one to you.

"This is the first glint of hope I've had since the attack failed, and I owe it to you. And now, Jim, we're to go in for this here treasure hunting, with sealed orders, too. And I don't like it. You and me must stick close, back to back, like. We'll save our necks in spite o' fate and fortune."

Just then a man called to us from the fire that breakfast was ready. We were soon seated here and there about the sand over biscuit and fried bacon. They had lit a fire fit to roast an ox. It was now grown so hot that they could only approach it from the windward, and even there not without extreme care.

In the same wasteful spirit, I suppose, they had cooked three times more than we could eat. One of them threw what was left into the fire with an empty laugh. The flames blazed and roared again over this unusual fuel.

I never in my life saw men so careless of the future. Hand to mouth is the only word that can describe their way of doing, what with wasted food and sleeping guards. They were bold enough for a brush and be done with it. But I could see their complete unfitness for anything like a **prolonged** campaign.

Even Silver—eating away with Captain Flint upon his shoulder—had not a word of blame for their recklessness. And this surprised me the more, for I thought he'd never shown himself so **cunning** as he did then.

"Ay, mates," said Silver, "it's lucky you have Barbecue to think for you with this here head. I got what I wanted, I did. Sure enough, they have the ship. Where they have it, I don't know yet. But once we hit the treasure, we'll have to jump about and find out. And then, mates, us that has the boats has the upper hand, I reckon."

Thus he kept running on, with his mouth full of the hot bacon. Thus he restored their hope and confidence. I more than suspect he repaired his own at the same time.

"As for hostage," he continued, "I guess that's his last talk with them he loves so dear. I've got my piece o' news and thanky to him for that. But it's over and done. I'll tie him on a line when we go treasure hunting. In the meantime we'll keep him like so much gold, in case of accidents, you mark. Once we got the ship and treasure both, we'll be off to sea like jolly companions. Why, then we'll talk Mr. Hawkins over, we will. We'll give him his share for all his kindness, to be sure."

It was no wonder the men were in a good humor now. For my part, I felt horribly let down. Should the scheme he had now sketched prove **feasible,** Silver—already doubly a traitor—wouldn't hesitate to adopt it. He had still a foot in either camp. There was no doubt he wanted wealth and freedom with the pirates. He'd prefer that to a bare escape from hanging, which was the best he had to hope for on our side.

Nay, and even if things so fell out that he was forced to keep his faith with Dr. Livesey—even then what danger lay before us! What a moment that would be when the suspicions of his followers turned to certainty. He and I should have to fight for dear life—he a cripple and I a boy—against five strong and active seamen!

Add to this double apprehension the mystery that still hung over the behavior of my friends. There was their unexplained desertion of the stockade and their inexplicable giving up of the chart. Harder still to understand was the doctor's last warning to Silver, "Look out for trouble when you find it." You will readily believe how little taste I found in my breakfast. It was with an uneasy heart that I set forth behind my captors on the quest for treasure.

We made a strange sight, had anyone been there to see us. We were all in soiled sailor clothes, and all but me were armed to the teeth. Silver had two guns slung about him—one before and one behind. He also had the great cutlass at his waist and a pistol in each pocket of his square-tailed coat. To complete Silver's strange appearance, Captain Flint sat perched upon his shoulder gabbling odds and ends of meaningless sea talk.

I had a line about my waist and followed obediently after the sea cook. Silver held the loose end of the rope, now in his free hand, now between his powerful teeth. For all the world, I was led like a dancing bear.

The other men were burdened in their own way. Some carried picks and shovels, for that had been the very first necessity they brought ashore from the *Hispaniola.* Others were loaded down with pork, bread, and brandy for the midday meal. All the stores came from our stock, I observed.

I could see the truth of Silver's words the night

before. Had he not struck a bargain with the doctor? He and the mutineers—deserted by the ship—would have been driven to **subsist** on clear water and whatever they could get from hunting. Water would have been little to their taste. And a sailor isn't usually a good shot. Besides all that, when they were so short of eatables it wasn't likely they would be very well stocked with powder.

Well, thus equipped, we all set out. Even the fellow with the broken head went with us. He certainly should have kept in the shade. We straggled one after another to the beach where the two gigs awaited us. Even these bore traces of the drunken folly of the pirates. One had a broken seat. And both were in a muddied and unbaled condition. Both were to be carried along with us for the sake of safety. So with our numbers divided between, we set forth upon the bosom of the anchorage.

As we pulled over, there was some discussion about the chart. The red cross was far too large to be a guide, of course. The terms of the note on the back admitted of some vagueness, as you will hear. The reader may remember they ran thus:

> "Tall tree, Spy-glass Shoulder, bearing a point
> to the N. of N.N.E.
>   Skeleton Island E.S.E. and by E.
>   Ten feet."

A tall tree was thus the **principal** mark. Now right before us, the anchorage was bounded by a plateau[1] from two to three hundred feet high. The plateau joined on the north with the sloping southern shoulder of the Spy-glass. Then it rose again towards the south into the rough, cliffy rise called the Mizzen-mast Hill.

The top of the plateau was dotted thickly with pine trees of different heights. Every here and there, one of a different species rose forty or fifty feet clear above its neighbors. Which of these was the particular "tall tree" of Captain Flint could only be decided on the spot and by the readings of the compass.

---

[1] A plateau is a high, level expanse of land.

Yet, although that was the case, every man on board the boats had picked a favorite of his own before we were halfway over. Long John alone shrugged his shoulders and told them to wait until they were there.

By Silver's directions we pulled easily, so as not to weary the hands too soon. After quite a long passage, we landed at the mouth of the second river—that which runs down a woody cleft of the Spy-glass. Then, bending to our left, we began to climb up the slope towards the plateau.

At first, heavy, muddy ground and a matted, marshy vegetation greatly delayed our progress. But little by little the hill began to get steeper and become stony underfoot. The woods began to change its character and to grow in a more open order.

Indeed, it was a most pleasant part of the island that we were now approaching. Heavy-scented bushes and many flowering shrubs had almost taken the place of grass. Thickets of green nutmeg trees were dotted here and there with the red columns and the broad shadow of the pines. The first mixed their spice with the scent of the others. The air was fresh and stirring, besides. Under the bright sunbeams, this was a wonderful refreshment to our senses.

The party spread itself abroad in a fan shape, shouting and leaping to and fro. About the center and a good way behind the rest, Silver and I followed. I was **tethered** by my rope. He ploughed through the sliding gravel with deep pants. Indeed, from time to time I had to lend him a hand. Otherwise he might have missed his footing and fallen backward down the hill.

We had thus proceeded for about half a mile. We were approaching the brow of the plateau when the man on the farthest left began to cry aloud, as if in terror. Shout after shout came from him. The others began to run in his direction.

"He can't 'a' found the treasure," said old Morgan, hurrying past us from the right. "That's clean a-top."

Indeed, as we found when we also reached the spot, it was something very different. At the foot of a pretty big pine a human skeleton lay with a few shreds of clothing on the ground. The skeleton was tangled up in a green vine, which had even partly lifted some of the smaller bones. I believe that for a moment a chill struck at every heart.

"He was a seaman," said George Merry. Bolder than the rest, he had gone up close and was examining the rags of clothing. "At any rate, this is good sea cloth."

"Aye, aye," said Silver, "like enough. You wouldn't look to find a bishop[2] here, I reckon. But what sort of a way is that for bones to lie? 'Tain't natural."

Indeed, on a second glance, it seemed impossible to imagine that the body was in a natural position. Except for some **disarray,** the man lay perfectly straight. His feet pointed in one direction. His hands were raised above his head like a diver's, pointing directly in the opposite. However, it looked as if birds had fed upon him. And the growing vine had gradually wrapped around his remains.

"I've taken an idea into my old numbskull," observed Silver. "Here's the compass. There's the tip-top point o' Skeleton Island, stickin' out like a tooth. Just take a bearing along the line of them bones, will you?"

It was done. The body pointed straight in the direction of the island. The compass read duly E.S.E. and by E.

"I thought so," cried the cook. "This here is a pointer. Right up there is our line for the Pole Star and the jolly dollars. But, by thunder! If it don't make me cold inside to think of Flint. This is one of *his* jokes, and no mistake. Him and these six was alone here. He killed 'em, every man. And this one he hauled here and laid down by compass, shiver my timbers! They're long bones and the hair's been yellow. Ay, that would be Allardyce. You remember Allardyce, Tom Morgan?"

"Aye, aye" replied Morgan. "I remember him. He

---

[2] A bishop is a high-ranking Christian clergyman.

owed me money, he did. And he took my knife ashore
with him."

"Speaking of knives," said another, "why don't we
find his lying round? Flint warn't the man to pick a
seaman's pocket. And the birds would leave it be, I
guess."

"By the powers and that's true!" cried Silver.

"There ain't a thing left here," said Merry, still feeling
round among the bones. "Not a copper coin nor a
tobacco box. It don't look natural to me."

"No, by gum, it don't," agreed Silver. "Not natural,
nor not nice, says you. Great guns, messmates! But if
Flint was living, this would be a hot spot for you and me.
Six they were and six are we. And bones is what they are
now."

"I saw Flint dead with these here eyes," said Morgan.
"Billy took me in. There he laid, with penny pieces on his
eyes."

"Dead—aye, sure enough he's dead and gone below,"
said the fellow with the bandage. "But if ever a spirit
walked, it would be Flint's. Dear heart, but he died bad,
did Flint!"

"Aye, that he did," observed another. "Now he raged
and now he hollered for the rum and now he sang.
'Fifteen Men' were his only song, mates. It was main hot
and the window was open. I heard that old song comin'
out as clear as clear—and the death-haul on the man
already. I tell you true, I never rightly liked to hear it
since."

"Come, come," said Silver, "stop this talk. He's dead
and he don't walk, that I know. Anyway, he won't walk by
day, and you may lay to that. Care killed a cat. Fetch
ahead for the doubloons."

We started, certainly. But in spite of the hot sun and
the staring daylight, the pirates no longer ran separate
and shouting through the woods. They kept side by side
and spoke with bated breath. The terror of the dead
buccaneer had fallen on their spirits.

Chapter 32

The Treasure Hunt—The Voice Among the Trees

> ### Vocabulary Preview
>
> The following words appear in this chapter. Review the list and get to know the words before you read the chapter.
>
> **conspicuous**—noticeable; visible
> **damping**—depressing; discouraging
> **excavation**—hole or pit made by digging
> **extravagance**—overspending; having more than one needs
> **irreverence**—disrespect; scorn
> **superstitious**—those who believe in magic or chance

Partly from the **damping** influence of this alarm, partly to rest Silver and the sick folk, the whole party sat down as soon as they had gained the top of the hill.

The plateau was somewhat tilted towards the west. So this spot on which we had paused gave us a wide view on either hand. Before us over the treetops, we beheld the Cape of the Woods fringed with surf. Behind we looked down upon the anchorage and Skeleton Island. And we saw—clear across the spit and the eastern lowlands—a great field of open sea on the east.

Straight above us rose the Spy-glass. Here it was dotted with single pines, there black with precipices.[1] There was no sound but that of the distant breakers, mounting from all round. That, and the chirp of countless

[1] Precipices are steep cliffs.

insects in the brush. Not a man, not a sail was upon the sea. The very largeness of the view increased the sense of loneliness.

As he sat, Silver took certain bearings with his compass.

"There are three 'tall trees' about in the right line from Skeleton Island," he said. "I take it 'Spy-glass Shoulder' means that lower point there. It's child's play to find the stuff now. I've half a mind to dine first."

"I don't feel sharp," growled Morgan. "Thinkin' o' Flint—I think it were—has done me."

"Ah, well, my son, you praise your stars he's dead," said Silver.

"He were an ugly devil," cried a third pirate with a shudder. "And blue in the face, too!"

"That was how the rum took him," added Merry. "Blue! Well, I reckon he was blue. That's a true word."

Ever since they had found the skeleton and got upon this train of thought, they had spoken lower and lower. They had almost got to whispering by now. The sound of their talk hardly interrupted the silence of the woods. All of a sudden we heard something out of the middle of the trees in front of us. It was a thin, high, trembling voice. And this voice struck up the well-known tune and words:

> *"Fifteen men on the dead man's chest—*
> *Yo-ho-ho, and a bottle of rum!"*

I've never seen men more dreadfully affected than the pirates. The color went like magic from their six faces. Some leaped to their feet. Some clawed hold of others. Morgan squirmed on the ground.

"It's Flint, by—!" cried Merry.

The song had stopped as suddenly as it began. It was broken off in the middle of a note, you would have said. It was as though someone had laid his hand upon the singer's mouth. The sound had come far through the clear, sunny atmosphere among the green treetops. I thought it had sounded airily and sweetly. The effect on my companions was all the stranger.

"Come," said Silver, struggling with his white lips to get the word out. "This won't do. Stand by to go about. This is a rum start. I can't name the voice, but it's someone skylarking—someone that's flesh and blood, and you may lay to that."

His courage had come back as he spoke, and some of the color to his face along with it. Already the others had begun to lend an ear to this encouragement and were coming a little to themselves. Then the same voice broke out again—this time not singing. It spoke in a faint, distant call that echoed even fainter among the clefts of the Spy-glass.

"Darby M'Graw," it wailed—for that's the word that best describes the sound. "Darby M'Graw! Darby M'Graw!" Again and again and again, then rising a little higher and with an oath that I leave out, "Fetch aft the rum, Darby!"

The buccaneers remained rooted to the ground, their eyes starting from their heads. Long after the voice had died away, they still stared in silence, dreadfully, before them.

"That fixes it!" gasped one. "Let's go."

"They was his last words," moaned Morgan. "His last words above board."

Dick had his Bible out and was praying with quick words. He had been well brought up, had Dick. That was before he came to sea and fell among bad companions.

Still, Silver was unconquered. I could hear his teeth rattle in his head, but he hadn't yet surrendered.

"Nobody in this here island ever heard of Darby," he muttered. "Not one but us that's here." And then, making a great effort, he cried, "Shipmates! I'm here to get that stuff. I'll not be beat by man nor devil. I never was scared of Flint in his life. And by the powers, I'll face him dead.

"There's seven hundred thousand pounds less than a quarter of a mile from here," said Silver. "When did a gentleman o' fortune ever show his stern to that much

dollars? Not for a boozy old seaman with a blue mug—
and him dead, too."

But there was no sign of renewed courage in his
followers. Rather, indeed, there was growing terror at the
irreverence of his words.

"Hold it there, John!" said Merry. "Don't you cross a
spirit."

And the rest were all too terrified to reply. They
would have run away separately had they dared. But fear
kept them together and kept them close by Silver, as if his
daring helped them. He on his part had pretty well fought
his weakness down.

"Spirit? Well, maybe," he said. "But there's one thing
not clear to me. There was an echo. Now, no man ever
seen a spirit with a shadow. Well, then, what's he doing
with an echo to him, I should like to know? Surely that
ain't natural?"

This argument seemed weak enough to me. But you
can never tell what will affect the **superstitious.** To my
wonder, George Merry was greatly relieved.

"Well, that's so," he said. "You've a head upon your
shoulders, John, and no mistake. About ship, mates! This
here crew is on a wrong tack, I do believe. And come to
think on it, it was like Flint's voice, I grant you. But it
wasn't just so clear away like it, after all. It was more like
somebody else's voice now—it was more like—"

"By the powers, Ben Gunn!" roared Silver.

"Ay, and so it were," cried Morgan, springing on his
knees. "Ben Gunn it were!"

"It don't make much odds, do it now?" asked Dick.
"Ben Gunn's not here in the body, any more'n Flint."

But the older hands greeted this remark with scorn.

"Why, nobody minds Ben Gunn," cried Merry. "Dead
or alive, nobody minds him."

It was extraordinary how their spirits had returned.
The natural color had returned to their faces. Soon they
were chatting together, stopping every now and then to
listen. Not long after—hearing no further sound—they

shouldered the tools and set forth again.

Merry walked first with Silver's compass to keep them on the right line with Skeleton Island. He had said the truth. Dead or alive, nobody minded Ben Gunn.

Dick alone still held his Bible and looked around him as he went, with fearful glances. But he found no sympathy. Silver even teased him on his precautions.

"I told you," said he, "I told you, you had spoiled your Bible! If it ain't no good to swear by, what do you suppose a spirit would give for it? Not that!" And he snapped his big fingers, halting a moment on his crutch.

But Dick wasn't to be comforted. Indeed, it was soon plain to me that the lad was falling sick. The fever predicted by Doctor Livesey was evidently growing swiftly higher. It was quickened by heat, exhaustion, and the shock of his alarm.

It was fine open walking here upon the summit. Our way lay a little downhill, for the plateau tilted towards the west, as I've said. The pines, great and small, grew wide apart. Even between the clumps of nutmeg and azalea,[2] wide open spaces baked in the hot sunshine.

We struck pretty near northwest across the island. We drew ever nearer the shoulders of the Spy-glass on the one hand. On the other, we looked ever wider over that western bay where I had once tossed and trembled in the coracle.

The first of the tall trees was reached. By the bearing, it proved to be the wrong one. So with the second. The third rose nearly two hundred feet in the air above a clump of underbrush. It was a giant of a vegetable, with a red column as big as a cottage. A company[3] could have moved about in its wide shadow. The tree was **conspicuous** far out to sea both on the east and west. It might well have been entered as a sailing mark upon the chart.

But it wasn't the tree's size that now impressed my

---

[2] An azalea is a shrub with showy flowers.
[3] A company is a group of soldiers.

companions. It was the knowledge that seven hundred thousand pounds in gold lay somewhere buried beneath its spreading shadow. As they drew nearer, the thought of the money swallowed up their previous terrors. Their eyes burned in their heads. Their feet grew speedier and lighter. Their whole soul was bound up in that fortune, in the whole lifetime of **extravagance** and pleasure that lay waiting there for each of them.

Silver hobbled on his crutch, grunting. His nostrils stood out and quivered. He cursed like a madman when the flies settled on his hot and shiny face. He plucked furiously at the line that held me to him. From time to time, he turned his eyes upon me with a deadly look.

Certainly, Silver took no pains to hide his thoughts. And certainly I read them like print. In the immediate nearness of the gold, all else had been forgotten. His promise and the doctor's warning were both things of the past.

I couldn't doubt that Silver hoped to seize upon the treasure. He'd find and board the *Hispaniola* under cover of night. He'd cut every honest throat about that island. Then he'd sail away as he had at first intended, weighed down with crimes and riches.

Shaken as I was with these alarms, it was hard for me to keep up with the rapid pace of the treasure hunters. Now and again I stumbled. It was then that Silver plucked so roughly at the rope and threw his murderous glances at me.

Dick had dropped behind us and now brought up the rear. He was babbling to himself both prayers and curses, as his fever kept rising. This also added to my misery. To top it all, I was haunted by the thought of the tragedy that had once been acted on that plateau.

That ungodly buccaneer with the blue face—he who died at Savannah, singing and shouting for drink—had cut down his six accomplices there, with his own hand. This grove that was now so peaceful must then have rung with cries, I thought. Even with the thought, I could believe I heard it ringing still.

We were now at the margin of the thicket.

"Huzza, mates, altogether!" shouted Merry, and the ones in front broke into a run.

And suddenly, not ten yards farther, we saw them stop. A low cry arose. Silver doubled his pace, digging away with the foot of his crutch like one possessed. Next moment, he and I had also come to a dead halt.

Before us was a great **excavation.** It wasn't very recent, for the sides had fallen in and grass had sprouted on the bottom. In this were the shaft of a pick broken in two and the boards of several packing cases scattered around. On one of these boards, I saw branded with a hot iron the name *Walrus*—the name of Flint's ship.

All was clear to see. The cache had been found and rifled. The seven hundred thousand pounds were gone!

Chapter 33

The Fall of a Chieftain

Vocabulary Preview

The following words appear in this chapter. Review the list and get to know the words before you read the chapter.

amassing—gathering; collecting
cordial—friendly; warm
dereliction—neglect; failure
dispatched—sent to perform an errand or duty
escapade—wild adventure
insolence—rudeness; disrespect

There never was such an upset in this world. Each of these six men was as though he had been struck. But with Silver, the blow passed almost instantly. Every thought of his soul had been set full-stretch like a racer on that money. Well, he was brought up in a single second, dead. He kept his head and found his temper. Silver had changed his plan before the others had time to realize the disappointment.

"Jim," he whispered, "take that and stand by for trouble."

And he passed me a double-barreled pistol.

At the same time, he began quietly moving northward. In a few steps he had put the hollow between us two and the other five. Then he looked at me and nodded, as much as to say, "Here's a narrow corner." As indeed, I thought it was. Silver's looks were now quite friendly. I was so disgusted at these constant changes that I couldn't help whispering, "So you've changed sides again."

There was no time left for him to answer. With oaths and cries, the buccaneers began to leap one after another into the pit. They dug with their fingers, throwing the boards aside as they did so. Morgan found a piece of gold. He held it up with a perfect stream of oaths. It was a two-guinea piece. It went from hand to hand among them for a quarter of a minute.

"Two guineas!" roared Merry, shaking it at Silver. "That's your seven hundred thousand pounds, is it? You're the man for bargains, ain't you? You're him that never bungled nothing, you wooden-headed lubber!"

"Dig away, boys," said Silver, with the coolest **insolence.** "You'll find some pig-nuts[1] and I shouldn't wonder."

"Pig-nuts!" repeated Merry, in a scream. "Mates, do you hear that? I tell you, now, that man there knew it all along. Look in the face of him and you'll see it written there."

"Ah, Merry," remarked Silver, "standing for cap'n again? You're a pushing lad, to be sure."

But this time everyone was entirely in Merry's favor. They began to scramble out of the excavation, shooting furious glances behind them. One thing I observed that looked well for us: they all got out upon the opposite side from Silver.

Well there we stood, two on one side, five on the other, the pit between us. Nobody was screwed up high enough to offer the first blow. Silver never moved. He watched them, very upright on his crutch, and looked as cool as ever I saw him. He was brave, and no mistake.

At last, Merry seemed to think a speech might help matters.

"Mates," says he, "there's two of them alone there.

[1] Pig nuts are bitter-tasting hickory nuts.

One's the old cripple that brought us all here and blundered us down to this. The other's that cub I mean to have the heart of. Now, mates—"

He was raising his arm and his voice and plainly meant to lead a charge. But just then—crack! crack! crack!—three musket shots flashed out of the thicket. Merry tumbled headfirst into the excavation. The man with the bandage spun round like a top and finally fell upon his side. There he lay, dead but still twitching. The other three turned and ran for it with all their might.

Before you could wink, Long John had fired two barrels of a pistol into the struggling Merry. The man rolled up his eyes at Silver in the last agony.

"George," Silver said, "I reckon I settled you."

At the same moment, the doctor, Gray, and Ben Gunn joined us with smoking muskets from among the nutmeg trees.

"Forward!" cried the doctor. "Double quick, my lads. We must head 'em off the boats."

And we set off at a great pace, sometimes plunging through the bushes to our chest.

I tell you, but Silver was anxious to keep up with us. The work that man went through was work no sound man ever equaled. He leaped on his crutch till the muscles on his chest were fit to burst. So thinks the doctor, too. As it was, he was already thirty yards behind us, and on the verge of strangling, when we reached the edge of the slope.

"Doctor," he called. "See there! No hurry!"

Sure enough there was no hurry. In a more open part of the plateau, we could see the three survivors. They were still running in the same direction as they had started, right for Mizzen-mast Hill. We were already between them and the boats. So we four sat down to breathe. Long John came slowly up with us, mopping his face.

"Thank ye kindly, doctor," says he. "You came in about the nick of time for me and Hawkins, I guess. And so it's you, Ben Gunn!" he added. "Well, you're a nice one, to be sure."

"I'm Ben Gunn, I am," replied the marooned man, wriggling like an eel in his embarrassment. "And," he added, after a long pause, "how do, Mr. Silver? Pretty well, I thank ye, says you."

"Ben, Ben," murmured Silver, "to think as you've done me!"

The doctor sent back Gray for one of the pickaxes deserted by the mutineers in their flight. Then we proceeded leisurely downhill to where the boats were lying. The doctor related in a few words what had taken place. It was a story that greatly interested Silver. And Ben Gunn, the half-idiot maroon, was the hero from beginning to end.

Ben had found the skeleton in his lonely wanderings about the island. It was he that had robbed it. He had found the treasure. He had dug it up (it was the handle of his pickaxe that lay broken in the excavation). He had carried it on his back in many weary journeys to another hiding place.

Ben had moved the treasure from the foot of the tall pine to a cave he had on the two-pointed hill at the northeast angle of the island. There it had lain stored in safety since two months before the *Hispaniola* arrived.

The doctor had wormed this secret from him on the afternoon of the attack. When next morning he saw the anchorage deserted, he had gone to Silver. The doctor had given Silver the chart, which was now useless. He had also given him the stores, for Ben Gunn's cave was well supplied with goat's meat salted by Ben himself.

The doctor had given anything and everything to get a chance of moving in safety from the stockade to the two-pointed hill. There they could be clear of malaria and keep a guard upon the money.

"As for you, Jim," Dr. Livesey said, "it went against my heart. But I did what I thought best for those who had stood by their duty. And if you weren't one of these, whose fault was it?"

That morning he found that I was to be involved in the horrid disappointment he had prepared for the mutineers. He had run all the way back to the cave. Leaving squire to guard the captain, the doctor had taken Gray and the maroon. They started out—making the diagonal across the island—to be at hand beside the pine.

Soon, however, he saw that our party was ahead of him. Ben Gunn, being fleet of foot, had been **dispatched** to do his best alone. Then it had occurred to Ben to work upon the superstitions of his former shipmates. He was so far successful that Gray and the doctor had caught up. They were already hidden before the arrival of the treasure hunters.

"Ah," said Silver, "it were fortunate for me that I had Hawkins here. You would have let old John be cut to bits and never given it a thought, doctor."

"Not a thought," replied Doctor Livesey cheerfully.

By this time we had reached the gigs. The doctor demolished one of them with the pickaxe. Then we all got aboard the other and set out to go round by sea for North Inlet.

This was a run of eight or nine miles. Silver was set to an oar like the rest of us, though he was almost killed already with fatigue. We were soon skimming swiftly over a smooth sea. Soon we passed out of the straits and turned the southeast corner of the island. It was round that corner that we had towed the *Hispaniola* four days ago.

As we passed the two-pointed hill, we could see the black mouth of Ben Gunn's cave. A figure was standing by it, leaning on a musket. It was the squire. We waved a handkerchief and gave him three cheers. Silver's voice joined as heartily as any.

Three miles farther, just inside the mouth of North Inlet, what should we meet but the *Hispaniola* cruising by herself! The last flood had lifted her. Had there been much wind or a strong current as in the southern anchorage, we should never have found her again. Or else we would have found her stranded beyond help.

As it was, there was little amiss except for the wreck of the mainsail. Another anchor was got ready and dropped in a fathom and a half of water. We all pulled round again to Rum Cove, the nearest point for Ben Gunn's treasure house. Then Gray returned alone with the gig to the *Hispaniola.* He was to pass the night there on guard.

A gentle slope ran up from the beach to the entrance of the cave. At the top, the squire met us. To me he was **cordial** and kind. He said nothing of my **escapade,** either in the way of blame or praise. At Silver's polite salute, the squire somewhat flushed.

"John Silver," he said, "you're an outrageous villain and imposter—a monstrous imposter, sir. I'm told I am not to prosecute you. Well, then, I will not. But the dead men hang about your neck like millstones,[2] sir."

"Thank you kindly, sir," replied Long John, again saluting.

"I dare you to thank me!" cried the squire. "It is a great **dereliction** of my duty. Stand back."

And thereupon we all entered the cave. It was a large, airy place. There was a little spring and a pool of clear water overhung with ferns. The floor was sand. Before a big fire lay Captain Smollett. In a far corner I beheld great heaps of coins and gold bars. They were only dimly flickered over by the blaze.

That was Flint's treasure that we had come so far to seek. It had cost already the lives of seventeen men from the *Hispaniola.* How many had it cost in the **amassing—** what blood and sorrow, what good ships scuttled on the deep? What brave men walking the plank blindfolded, what shot of cannon, what shame and lies and cruelty? Perhaps no man alive could tell. Yet there were still three upon that island—Silver and old Morgan and Ben

---

[2] Millstones are round stones used for the grinding of grain. The top stone has a hole in the center. The expression *dead men hang about your neck like millstones* means that Silver is responsible for the deaths of those men.

Gunn—who had each taken his share in these crimes. And each of them had hoped in vain to share in the reward.

"Come in, Jim," said the captain. "You're a good boy in your line, Jim. But I don't think you and me'll go to sea again. You're too much of the born favorite for me. Is that you, John Silver? What brings you here, man!"

"Come back to my duty, sir," replied Silver.

"Ah!" said the captain. And that was all he said.

What a supper I had of it that night, with all my friends around me. And what a meal it was, with Ben Gunn's salted goat and some delicacies and a bottle of old wine from the *Hispaniola!* I am sure no people were ever gayer or happier.

And there was Silver, sitting back almost out of the firelight but eating heartily. He was ready to spring forward when anything was wanted. He even joined quietly in our laughter—the same mild, polite, agreeable seaman of the voyage out.

Chapter 34

And Last

Vocabulary Preview

The following words appear in this chapter. Review the list and get to know the words before you read the chapter.

diversity—variety; difference
ingratiate—get on someone's good side; make friends with
onslaught—invasion; fierce attack
sojourn—short stay

The next morning we fell early to work. The transportation of this great mass of gold was a considerable task for so small a number of workmen. It was near a mile by land to the beach and from there three miles by boat to the *Hispaniola*.

The three fellows still abroad upon the island didn't greatly trouble us. A single guard on the shoulder of the hill was sufficient to insure us against any sudden **onslaught.** We thought besides that they had had more than enough of fighting.

Therefore the work pushed on briskly. Gray and Ben Gunn came and went with the boat. During their absences the rest piled treasure on the beach. Two of the bars slung in a rope's-end made a good load for a grown man—one that he was glad to walk slowly with. For my part, I wasn't much use at carrying. I was kept busy all day in the cave, packing the minted money into bread bags.

It was a strange collection for the **diversity** of coinage. It was somewhat like Billy Bones' hoard. But this was so much larger and so much more varied that I think I never had more pleasure than in sorting them.

There were English, French, Spanish, Portuguese, Georges, and Louises, doubloons and double guineas and moidores and sequins.[1] They carried the pictures of all the kings of Europe for the last hundred years. Some strange Oriental pieces were stamped with what looked like wisps of string or bits of spider's web. There were round pieces and square pieces and pieces bored through the middle as if to wear them round your neck.

I think nearly every variety of money in the world must have found a place in that collection. For number, I'm sure they were like autumn leaves. My back ached with stooping and my fingers ached with sorting them out.

Day after day this work went on. By every evening a fortune had been stowed aboard, but there was another fortune waiting for the next day. And all this time, we heard nothing of the three surviving mutineers.

At last—I think it was on the third night—the doctor and I were strolling on the shoulder of the hill where it overlooks the lowlands of the isle. From out of the thick darkness below, the wind brought us a noise between shrieking and singing. It was only a snatch that reached our ears, followed by the previous silence.

"Heaven forgive them," said the doctor. " 'Tis the mutineers!"

"All drunk, sir," struck in the voice of Silver from behind us.

Silver was allowed his entire liberty, I should say. In spite of daily put-downs, he seemed to regard himself once more as quite a privileged and friendly dependent. Indeed, it was remarkable how well he bore these snubs. With untiring politeness he kept on trying to **ingratiate**

---

[1] Georges are British half-crowns. Louises were French gold coins. Moidores were gold coins from Portugal and Brazil. Sequins were gold coins from Turkey.

himself with all.

Yet I think none treated Silver better than a dog. Not unless it was Ben Gunn, who was still terribly afraid of his old quartermaster. Or unless it was myself, who had really something to thank him for. Although for that matter, I suppose I had reason to think even worse of him than anybody else. I had seen him planning a fresh treachery upon the plateau.

Accordingly, it was pretty gruffly that the doctor answered Silver. "Drunk or raving," said he.

"Right you were, sir," replied Silver, "and precious little difference which it is, to you and me."

"I suppose you would hardly ask me to call you a humane man," replied the doctor with a sneer. "And so my feelings may surprise you, Master Silver. But if I were sure they were raving—as I am morally certain at least one of them is down with fever—I should leave this camp. At whatever risk to my own body, I would take them the aid of my skill."

"Ask your pardon, sir, you'd be very wrong," said Silver. "You would lose your precious life, and you may lay to that. I'm on your side now, hand and glove. I shouldn't wish for to see the party weakened, let alone yourself. Especially seeing as I know what I owes you. But these men down there, they couldn't keep their word—no, not supposing they wished to. What's more, they couldn't believe that you could."

"No," said the doctor. "You're the man to keep your word, we know that."

Well, that was about the last news we had of the three pirates. Only once we heard a gunshot a great way off and supposed them to be hunting. A council was held and it was decided that we must desert them on the island—to the huge glee of Ben Gunn and with the strong approval of Gray, I must say.

We left the mutineers a good stock of powder and shot, most of the salt goat, a few medicines, and some other necessities. We left tools, clothing, a spare sail, and a fathom or two of rope. And, by the particular desire of the doctor, we left a handsome present of tobacco.

That was about our last doing on the island. Before that, we had got the treasure stowed. We had shipped enough water and the remainder of the goat meat, in case of any distress. At last, one fine morning, we weighed anchor, which was about all we could manage. We stood out of North Inlet with the same colors flying that the captain had flown and fought under at the palisade.

The three fellows must have been watching us closer than we thought, as we soon proved. For coming through the narrows we had to lie very near the southern point. There we saw all three of them kneeling together on a spit of sand, with their arms raised in a plea.

I think it went to all our hearts to leave them in that wretched state. But we couldn't risk another mutiny. And to take them home for the gallows would have been a cruel sort of kindness. The doctor called out to them and told them of the stores we had left and where they were to find them. But they continued to call us by name. They appealed to us, for God's sake, to be merciful and not leave them to die in such a place.

At last, they saw that the ship still bore on her course and was now swiftly drawing out of earshot. One of them—I don't know which it was—leapt to his feet with a hoarse cry. He whipped his musket to his shoulder and set a shot whistling over Silver's head and through the mainsail.

After that, we kept under cover of the bulwarks. When I next looked out, they had disappeared from the spit. The spit itself had almost melted out of sight in the growing distance. That was the end of that, at least. Before noon, to my undescribable joy, the highest rock of Treasure Island had sunk into the blue round of sea.

We were so short of men that everyone on board had to give a hand—except for the captain lying on a mattress in the stern and giving his orders. Though greatly recovered, he was still in need of quiet. We laid the ship's head for the nearest port in Spanish America, for we couldn't risk the voyage home without fresh hands. As it was, what with baffling winds and a couple of fresh storms, we were all worn out before we reached it.

It was just at sundown when we cast anchor in a most beautiful landlocked gulf. We were immediately surrounded by shore boats full of Negroes and Mexican Indians and half-bloods. They were selling fruits and vegetables and offering to dive for bits of money.

We were glad for the sight of so many good-humored faces (especially the blacks), the taste of the tropical fruits, and above all, the lights that began to shine in the town. All these made a most charming contrast to our dark and bloody **sojourn** on the island.

The doctor and the squire, taking me along with them, went ashore to pass the early part of the night. Here they met the captain of an English man-of-war. They fell in talk with him and went aboard his ship. In short, they had such an agreeable time that day was breaking when we came alongside the *Hispaniola.*

Ben Gunn was on deck alone. As soon as we came on board, he began with wonderful twisting motions and expressions to make us a confession. Silver was gone. The old maroon had helped Silver escape in a shore boat some hours ago. Ben now assured us he had only done so to preserve our lives which would certainly have been forfeit if "that man with the one leg had stayed aboard."

But this wasn't all. The sea cook had not gone empty-handed. He had cut through a bulkhead unobserved. Silver had removed one of the sacks of coins worth perhaps three or four hundred guineas, to help him in his further wanderings.

I think we were all pleased to be so cheaply rid of him.

Well, to make a long story short, we got a few hands on board and made a good cruise home. The *Hispaniola* reached Bristol just as Mr. Blandly was beginning to think of fitting out her consort. Five men only of those who had sailed returned with her. "Drink and the devil had done for the rest," with a vengeance. Although, to be sure, we weren't quite in so bad a case as that other ship they sang about:

> *"With one man of her crew alive,*
> *What put to sea with seventy-five."*

All of us had an ample share of the treasure and used it wisely or foolishly, according to our natures. Captain Smollett is now retired from the sea. Gray not only saved his money, but was suddenly struck with the desire to improve himself. He studied his profession, and he is now mate and part owner of a fine full-rigged ship. He's married besides, and the father of a family.

As for Ben Gunn, he got a thousand pounds, which he spent or lost in three weeks. Or, to be more exact, in nineteen days, for he was back begging on the twentieth. Then he was given a lodge to keep, exactly as he had feared upon the island. He still lives, a great favorite with the country boys, though also the butt of many jokes with them. He is a notable singer in church on Sundays and saints' days.

Of Silver we have heard no more. That formidable seafaring man with one leg has at last gone clean out of my life. But I dare say he met his old Negress and perhaps still lives in comfort with her and Captain Flint. It is to be hoped so, I suppose. For his chances of comfort in another world are very small.

For all that I know, the bar silver and the arms still lie where Flint buried them. Certainly they shall lie there for me. Oxen and wain-ropes[2] wouldn't bring me back again to that accursed island. The worst dreams that ever I have are when I hear the surf booming about its coasts. Or when I start upright in bed with the sharp voice of Captain Flint still ringing in my ears: "Pieces of eight! Pieces of eight!"

THE END

[2] Wain-ropes are the ropes with which oxen tow a wagon.

Diagram of a Three-masted Schooner

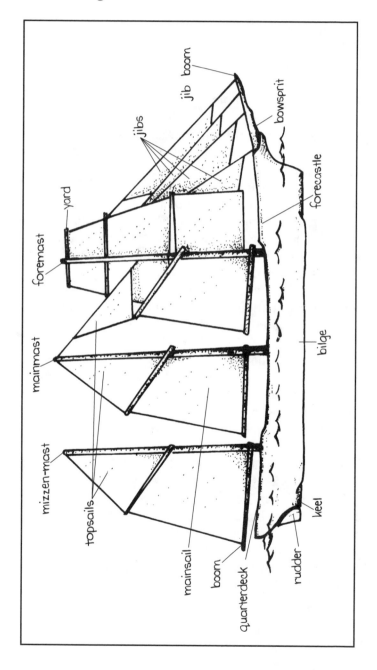

GLOSSARY OF NAUTICAL TERMS

afterdeck—back part of the deck; sometimes called *aft*

anchorage—place for a ship to drop its anchor

batten—seal shut

bearings—location based on compass directions; also, the part of an object that rests on a support

becalmed—motionless, due to lack of wind

bilge—lowest part inside a ship's hull; also refers to the dirty water that collects there

blocks—pulleys that tighten and hold the lines that control the sails

boatswain—ship's officer in charge of the hull; announces the captain's orders by playing signals on a pipe

booms—long poles that stretch out the bottom edge of a sail; connected to the poles supporting the sails; swing back and forth when the ship changes direction

bow—front of a boat or ship

bowsprit—wood or metal piece that extends forward from the front of a ship

broadside—side of a ship above the waterline

bulkhead—wall on a ship

bulwarks—sides of a ship that extend above the deck

bumboat—small boat that sells supplies to large ships

buoy—floating marker

capstan—thick post around which the anchor cable is wound; turned with spokes or bars at the top

careen—tilt a ship on one side so that the exposed side can be cleaned and repaired; must be done in shallow water or on a beach from which the ship can easily be floated again

catspaw—light wind that ruffles the surface of calm water

clove hitch—type of knot used by sailors; *in a clove hitch* is slang for "in a bind"

continued

companion—passageway between the ship's deck and the area below; also the hatch that covers that opening; also called *companionway*

coracle—boat made of waterproof material stretched over a lightweight wooden frame

coxswain—person who steers a boat or ship

cross-trees—horizontal crosspieces that spread the upper ropes in order to better support the mast

cutter—small, fast sailing ship, often used by the navy for patrol duties, especially close to the shore

cut-water—forward edge of a ship's hull

deadlights—shutters that close over the cabin windows on a ship; sailor slang for "eyes"

deck—ship's floor

dog watch—any of the guards' night shifts; in the novel, the dog watch refers to the last shift, which extended into early morning

fathom—unit of measurement equal to six feet; usually used to measure the depth of water

figurehead—carved image on the front of a ship

fog-horn—horn used in foggy weather to warn ships of rocks or other dangers

fore—front part of the deck

forecastle—forward part of a ship where the crew hands live; often spelled *fo'c'sle*

galley—ship's kitchen

gig—long, light ship's boat

hatch—opening in the deck of a ship

hawser—anchor rope or rope used to tie or tow a ship

helm—steering gear of a ship

hull—frame or body of a ship, not including the sails or masts

jib boom—extends forward from the bowsprit; the bottom corners of jibs are attached to the jib boom

jibs—triangular sails extending from the front of the foremast to the jib boom

jolly boat—medium-sized ship's boat used for general work

keel—lengthwise center structure at the bottom of a ship's frame

keel-hauling—dragging a person under a ship as punishment

larboard—as one faces forward on a ship, the left, or port, side

latitude—imaginary lines circling the globe; indicates the distance from the equator; exact location of a place can be determined by its latitude and longitude

lay to—bring a ship into the wind and hold it still; also, sailor slang for "keep still" or "be quiet"

lee—side of something protected from the wind

longitude—imaginary lines circling the globe; indicates distance east or west from Greenwich, England; the exact location of a place can be determined by its latitude and longitude

luff—shake; refers to the action of the sails when a ship heads into the wind; also refers to the act of purposely bringing the ship to face the wind

lugger—small ship with four-cornered sails

main—located near the mainmast or mainsail

mainmast—ship's principal, or main, sail

mainsail—largest sail on a ship, set on the mainmast

man-of-war—warship

mast—pole supporting the sails of a ship

mate—lower officer; term used also to mean a fellow worker or an equal

mizzen—third mast back on a sailing ship that has three or more masts; the sail on that mast

narrows—narrow body of water connecting two larger ones; also called *strait* or *straits*

nautical—related to or associated with the sea, sailors, or ships

continued

navigate—steer; sail over; control the course of something such as a ship

quarterdeck—rear area of a ship's upper deck

quartermaster—on a pirate ship, a person elected to represent the interests of the crew

quay—structure where ships can tie up and load or unload; also called *wharf*

reef—fold in a sail that takes up the sail to make it smaller

rigging—system of ropes and cables that control the masts and sails of a sailing ship

rudder—gear that controls the direction of a ship; on the *Hispaniola*, the rudder is controlled by a long rod called a *tiller*

schooner—sailing ship with two or more masts

scour—area scoured, or scrubbed, by a strong current of water

scupper holes—holes that allow water in the gutters to flow back into the sea

scuppers—gutters at the edge of the deck that drain water off

sea-calf—young walrus

shrouds—weblike set of lines that support the mast

skipper—ship captain

sounding—measurement of water depth

spar—wood or metal piece used as support for a ship's sails and ropes

starboard—as one faces forward on a ship, the right side

stays—heavy ropes or cables that brace a mast

straits—narrow body of water connecting two larger ones; also called *narrows*

swab—slang for "sailor"; also used as an insult to mean "worthless person"

tack—direction in which a ship moves, determined by the position of the sails

thwart—seat on a boat where the oarsman sits

tiller—long rod used to turn the rudder

top-sails—sails right above the lowest sail on a mast

trade winds—winds that blow almost constantly in one
   direction

wake—trail left on the water behind a moving ship

yard—long tapering pole attached crosswise to a mast;
   the top of a square-shaped sail is attached to the yard

yard-arm—either end of the yard; sometimes used as a
   gallows for hanging

younker—junior seaman